Chili Run

by

Stuart R. West

Copyright Notice
This is a work of fiction. Names, characters, places, and incidents are either the product of the author's imagination or are used fictitiously, and any resemblance to actual persons living or dead, business establishments, events, or locales, is entirely coincidental.

Chili Run

Contact Information: info@thewildrosepress.com

Cover Art by *Lea Schizas*

The Wild Rose Press, Inc.
PO Box 708
Adams Basin, NY 14410-0708
Visit us at www.thewildrosepress.com

Publishing History
First Edition, 2024
Trade Paperback ISBN 978-1-5092-5411-8
Digital ISBN 978-1-5092-5412-5
Previously Published April 2017

Published in the United States of America

Dedication

Everyone runs for something, usually something more important than chili. This book is dedicated to the dreamers and more importantly, the pursuers.

And, as always, huge thanks to Cydney for painstakingly driving me through the "mean streets" of Kansas City for research and Sarah for never running away from me.

Chapter One

6:30 P.M.

Drake tossed the beer across the room.

No surprise, Wendell dropped it, immensely thankful he'd opted to buy cans. He let it settle at his feet for a couple of seconds before pulling the tab. His costly studio walls didn't need a coat of lager.

"Smooth moves, bro." Drake commandeered the recliner by the window, Wendell's chair.

Better to just let Drake sit there, though. Years of failed conflict with his bigger brother, Drake, taught Wendell a hard truth: Drake had to win, absolutely had to win at everything. His preternatural extra rack of ribs always assured him a victory over Wendell's fragile frame.

"Still a wuss, brah," said Drake.

"Hey, my talents lie elsewhere." Beer in hand, false bravado in back pocket, Wendell settled into his dumpster-snatched sofa. He squirmed, trying to conform into the special spot between the springs which threatened to perforate the thread-bare upholstery. "I'm the armchair quarterback in the family." Longingly, Wendell glanced at his occupied armchair.

"Or something." Drake slurped at his can, brought it down in a weight-lifting jerk, and dragged his beefy arm across his mouth. "Ahhh!" As usual, everything amped up to steroidal levels. "So…these your new digs, huh?" He looked around, his loutish smirk clearly displaying disapproval. "Not exactly a palace, know what I mean?"

Wendell sighed, waited a beat—the safest course to navigate—before putting his thoughts into words. "Whatever. These are the trendiest up-and-coming studios in the KC Bottoms right now. Whole area's getting gentrified, every nook and cranny getting snatched up."

"I don't know much about trendy, you know, but you got the 'Bottoms' part right." He brayed at his little stab at humor. The sound effectively stabbed Wendell right between the eyes. "Looks like ass."

True, the studio was small, kinda ugly. Wendell never denied it. Ghastly green paint—the color only a mortician could appreciate—flaked away to expose faded brick walls, a "thing" to some people. Large pipes of an indefinable nature snaked up and crawled across the ceiling like rigid vines. Sudden cold drafts would grip Wendell with icy, ghostly fingers. And whenever his neighbor cut his toenails, Wendell heard the shrapnel hit the hardwood floors. But hey, the place had charm to burn. A little fixing up would make it quite appealing. Something Wendell intended to begin any day now. Soon. *Ish.*

"One man's 'ass' is another's treasure," offered Wendell. Of course, it made no sense. But if he polished his words up enough with simile, tied a bow of obfuscation around it, his cleverness would soar right over Drake's head. Sometimes it's the little victories that count.

"Yeah, but it still looks like ass, Wendy." Drake

blinked at his brother, dumbfounded, his typical expression declaring the end of the discussion.

"First of all, don't call me 'Wendy'. Second—" Wendell never reached his second point. Drake's ear-rending guffaws—similar to a helicopter dropping in—probably already had Wendell's neighbors calling 911.

Wendell rode it out, the way he did most things. Not chicken, not lazy, just always the smartest guy in a confrontation. Experience taught Wendell the smartest guy in a fight is the one who can run the fastest.

His tirade over, Drake drained his beer quickly. Jerkishness apparently made a man thirsty. His knot of an Adam's apple bounced up and down, everything about the guy testosterone unleashed. He crushed the can, then continued to crush Wendell's spirits.

"You know, when I heard you were moving to Kansas City to become a writer, this isn't what I imagined. Not at all."

Wendell figured Drake's imagination never extended further than Fantasy Football. "It is what it is, Drake. These are my writing digs."

"And how's that working out for you?"

For once, Wendell welcomed the outburst of noise outside. Seven p.m., right on time, the neighborhood thugs had gathered. Hoots and hollers and grunts—the way cavemen communicated—rose to Wendell's second-floor studio window. But, today, Wendell embraced the disruptive noise, anything to avoid his brother's incessant pushing regarding his writing career.

"What the hell is that?" Drake jerked his head toward the window. A cord—practically a rope—in his neck throbbed. Looked rather painful.

"Hmm? Oh, just the neighborhood boys having a little fun. Don't worry about it. I'll shut the window." Wendell scooted to the edge of the sofa, his bottom sunk deeper than his knees. He alley-ooped out of the man-trap and rushed toward the window to beat Drake before he did something stupid. As inevitable as death and taxes.

Too late. Drake stood. With a hand to Wendell's chest—and, man, did Wendell hate when Drake did that to him—Drake pushed Wendell back and pulled the curtain aside. "I'll be goddamned."

Below, gathered on the stoop of the building next door, four thugs jostled each other, shoving, shoulder punching, and shrieking like alley cats. As always, they gravitated toward the center of their galaxy: Big Ben. Ben sat on the steps, unusually quiet, something terrifying obviously swimming in his skull-shaved head. His cohorts must've smelled his foul mood as they gave him a wide berth, staying out of his immediate orbit. His attire remained the same, though, the only clothes Wendell had ever seen him in: sweatpants, t-shirt, a small fur stole draped around his massive shoulders, and a clock on a chain resting on his chest.

"What the hell is *this* crap?" Drake jut his hand outside the window, finger blatantly pointing at the neighborhood scare squad.

Wendell grabbed his arm, pulled it back inside. "Don't let 'em see you!"

"Damn, bro, get offa me!" Drake wrenched his arm away, and gifted Wendell with his furrow-browed finest. "Thought you said this was, I dunno, a hipster hang-out or somethin'."

"It is. They're just…hangers on from the old days. Before the neighborhood started climbing back up again. They'll be outta here soon. The law of nature." Wendell dangled a carrot he knew Drake couldn't refuse. "C'mon, let's get another brew."

Drake pursed his lips, mulled it over, finally saying, "Yeah, good idea."

Once Drake seized the armchair again, Wendell closed the window and rushed to the refrigerator. One eye on his brother, he retrieved another beer, and tossed it at Drake a la speedy delivery.

Click. Fsst. "Ahhhh!"

Wendell relaxed. Crisis averted. "Anyway…while you're here, Drake, I thought I'd take you to a couple micro-breweries, all within walking distance."

"Sounds good, sounds good… Any babes go there?"

"Oh, yeah. K.C.'s best." Not that Wendell knew too much about that, not really, but he gave a slow, knowing nod nonetheless.

"Now you're talkin' the language of love, brah. Hell, I was beginnin' to think—"

From outside, "*Hey! Don't chu' walk away when I'm talkin' to you!*"

"And the burgers at these places," continued Wendell, trying to drown out the commotion, "some of the best I've ever—"

"*Get your ass back here 'fore I put a cap in it!*"

"…had. Wait! You can't leave 'til you try the barbeque here! Man, I'm tellin' you…" Kicked into hyper-speed, Wendell spewed out a non-stop improvisational torrent of nonsense. Louder, faster, the power of an erupting vocal volcano. The way you'd distract a bratty child. Anything to keep his hot-headed brother from igniting the powder kegs on the stoop below. "…so *good* the meat practically *melts* off the bone and—"

"*That did it! I warned you! Your funeral, asshole!*"

"Oh, my *God*! You put up with this *crap* alla time?" Irate, Drake stood, tossed up the window. Through the narrow opening, he stuffed his square head and broad shoulders outside. "Hey! *Asshats*! Shut the *hell* up already!"

Wendell raced toward his brother. He grabbed Drake's arm, and wrenched him back inside. Wendell slammed the window, barricading it from Drake using his body as a human shield.

"You can't *do* that, Drake!"

Drake panted, a crazed look in his eyes. Nostrils of a rhinoceros. Fists coiled. Itching to fight. After only two beers. What the hell was Wendell thinking, plying him with beer?

"What the hell're you *doin'*? No one tells me what to *do*!" Drake squared his shoulders. Cracked his neck to further intimidate. Completely unnecessary.

"This isn't your regular barroom brawl, Drake! You *don't* wanna piss those guys off!"

"Ah, them? Fsss. Yeah, right…" He tossed out open palms. "What? All I did was tell those guys to shut up." All innocent and dumb now. Half of it was true.

"Exactly! And crap like that could get you—*us*—killed!"

"*What*? Come on!" Drake smirked as if suspicious Wendell was having one over on him. "I'm not afraid of them, bro! They're nothin' but—"

"Killers, drug dealers, psychos—"

"Get *out*. You scared of those guys?" Drake's thumb hitched back toward the window. "They're just some idiots tryin' to play big, bad 'gangsta.'"

"They're not playing." Solemnly, Wendell shook his head. "You see that guy out there, the one with the fur?"

Drake laughed. "The one with the clock? Yeah. What a dick."

"That 'dick's' name is Big Ben. He got that fur three weeks or so ago. Stole it off an old lady in his building. When he set fire to her studio. Medics carried out her charred, smoking body on a gurney."

"Right. Whatever, Wendy. Nothin' but a—whaddaya call it?—urban legend, that's what that is."

To be honest, Wendell didn't know for a fact Big Ben had started the fire. Just the scuttlebutt he'd heard around the neighborhood. But Wendell absolutely knew the fur belonged to the late Mrs. Haisley, saw her wearing it on her weekly strolls to the corner market. All of this would be lost on Drake, though, frustrating as putting together European furniture.

"Just listen to me for once, Drake. Leave them alone. Let's have a good time. A *safe* time."

"Bro, you're givin' into terrorism! That's what they want you to do! Sit here, cowering in your little trendy…" He threw out air quotes, his fingers thick as hot dogs. Wendell wondered how in hell his brother developed muscular fingers. "…studio. Don't give into 'em, bro!"

My God. How do you redirect a rhino?

"Ah, forget it. Turn the other cheek and all that. Hey, how 'bout another beer?"

This time, Drake didn't think twice, not that he did a bang-up job on his first round of thinking. "Cool, cool, cool. Let's drink!"

Before the Window of Doom could lead his brother astray again, Wendell tossed another beer from the refrigerator. "Think fast!"

Wendell knew his brother couldn't deny a challenge. Although Wendell's toss came up short, Drake dove for it, and remarkably caught it while dropping to his knees. He chugged a victory drink. "Ahhh! Still got it!"

And would never let Wendell forget it, either. But at least the fire had been put out.

Still, even with the window closed, Wendell'd always been able to hear the thugs outside during their nightly ribaldry. Now he heard nothing—a thick, soupy silence. A troublesome thought. What if they were coming to pay a visit?

Wendell offered a hand to pull Drake off the floor. Not that Drake needed it. He brushed his brother's hand away and kipped up into a squat, then hopped up like an Olympic gymnast, one arm imperiously extended to imaginary, adoring audience members.

Showoff.

While Drake basked in his own adulation, Wendell leaned over, and snuck a peek out the window. He saw nothing. On tiptoes, he strained to see farther as if he could view beyond the physical limitations of architecture. He saw enough. The stoop had been abandoned. His face practically smushed up against the window, he caught movement below him. Several hoodied arms flailed about as if in a heated argument. Yet they remained quiet, eerily so.

"What're they up to now, brah?" asked Drake.

"Hmm? Oh, nothing. Have a seat, let's chill."

But Wendell felt far from chill, other than the kind careening down his back. He imagined Big Ben setting fire to his apartment, blasting a cap into him, or shivving him during his morning jog (even though Wendell doubted the beasts rose before noon, why he chose the mornings for his runs). Worse, images of how far Big Ben might go played across his wide-screen mind-set. Disturbing images of what always happened to the quiet, nice guys in prison movies with Wendell ending up in make-up and hanging onto Big Ben's belt loop (*do sweatpants even have belt loops?*) and dammit, he really needed to quit watching those kinds of movies!

Perspiration trickled down from Wendell's hairline, an embarrassing trait. As he plastered on a falsely relaxed face, he thought the sweat might crack it in half.

"So…anyway…um, what were we talking about?" asked Wendell.

Drake rolled his beer can between his hands, his already short attention span challenged. Constantly, he glanced toward the window as if expecting something to happen. Wendell wished for the opposite; he desperately longed for the brick walls to close in and cut them off from so-called civilization.

"I dunno," said Drake. "Hey, what happened to your girlfriend? The one you told Mom and Dad about?"

Uh-oh. The second topic Wendell didn't wish to discuss with his brother.

"Ahhh…Alicia? Didn't work out. You

know…women.” Wendell blew it off, the way his brother might. If he had a caveman’s club, the sexist portrait would be complete. Wendell gladly traveled the low road, anything to avoid explaining how he’d been a bit hasty in proclaiming Alicia his girlfriend.

“I hear ya, I hear ya.” Drake said it hollowly, an artificial echo. He hadn’t heard him at all. But Wendell knew this constituted solid philosophy on his brother’s behalf.

“Hey! You got a problem or something?”

Dammit, round three. Immediately, Wendell recognized the sonorous voice of Big Ben, pitched so low only dogs and frightened people could hear it. Completely opposite his crew’s animated, shrieking tones. Not that Wendell’d ever personally crossed paths with Ben before, no sir. When it came to Big Ben, Wendell strove to maintain absolute invisibility. Yet, he’d heard all the men’s voices time and again, could pick them out of a line-up blindfolded and slap nametags on everyone.

“He talking to me?” Drake, rising to another challenge, obviously what he’d been waiting for, grinned. The scary kind of crazed grin Wendell recognized from childhood. “You think he’s talkin’ to me, bro?” Ape style, he thumped his chest.

“Come on, Drake, no way. They’ve moved on, probably talking to some—”

“Hey! Second floor! Talkin’ to you! You got somethin’ to say to me?”

“Oh, *hell* no!”

“Drake, don’t… Dammit, Drake, stop—”

The window slashed up with a heart-thumping clack. Drake poked his face out, burning red. “Hell, *yes*,

I got something to say to you! Shut the *hell* up, punk-ass!"

Giggles and taunts, a preamble to battle. Something clacked, something solid on metal. Weapons coming out.

"That ain't very nice." Simple, low-stated, very menacing, and one hundred percent Big Ben.

"Drake, that's *enough*. Just ignore them."

Head still outside, Drake nudged Wendell back with a finger, treating Wendell as if nothing more than a pesky gnat. "Nice? *Nice*?" called Drake out the window. "What is this? Preschool? You're the jackasses screamin' like you're little school girls!"

Crap.

Not only had Drake poked the bear, he'd sloshed gas in its eyes. "Dammit, Drake, get away from the window! Apologize to them!"

That got Drake's attention, not necessarily the kind Wendell wanted, either. Drake straightened, didn't even flinch when he banged his head on the windowsill. Flushed, his breath short and sharp, he said, "*Apologize*? You gotta be kidding me, Wendy! No way am I gonna—"

"Come on down! We'll sit, talk a spell, get *neighborly*." Big Ben's voice commanded attention—respect, even. So resonant, nearly charming. For a moment, Wendell considered a peace summit, a nice sit-down where all could be resolved. Then he wondered if Big Ben had huffed and puffed with a hidden wolf-like façade at Mrs. Hainsley's door.

"Like *hell* you wanna talk!" Drake back to egging them on. "Takes, what, *five* of you guys to take *me*? *Pussies*!"

Wendell cringed at the term. Not only because he'd suffered wounds from that particular vocal knife many times, but he also knew it'd cut Big Ben deep. Big Ben would cut deeper, though. *Much* deeper.

Below, the men hushed. Worse than an old-west gunfight, just waiting for Big Ben to chime high noon. Finally, Big Ben said, "*Bitch.*"

One word. The one that absolutely pulled Drake's trigger. Wendell knew it, knew it as sure as the sun would rise tomorrow, and now, that seemed like a 50-50 shot at best, at least for the Worthy brothers.

"You call me a bitch, *bitch*? I'm gonna kick *your* ass, and *your* ass, and your…" Drake pinpointed his targets like a starving man reading from a restaurant menu. Laughter fueled his rage. He swung around, practically hyperventilating. Fists coiled, unleashed, then wrapped up tight again. Sweat swamped his underarms.

"Drake, look, I know they're dicks. But they're dangerous—"

"You think *they're* dangerous? Little bro, you ain't *seen* the bloody trail!"

"I don't really want to either! Just please…stop for a minute, take a breath, then—"

"Uh-uh. They *punked* me! Called me a *bitch*! You believe that? *Me*! A bitch! I'm gonna show them somethin'!"

One last chance. Wendell blocked his brother's path. "I can't let you do that. They'll kill you! Mom and Dad would—"

"You gonna stop me?" Drake stepped up. Their nose tips touched, Drake's eyes melding into one cyclopean orb. Ready to kill the messenger.

Briefly, Wendell measured his options, limited as they were. Threaten to tell Mom and Dad? *No, ridiculous and weak.* Stop him by whatever physical means necessary? *Hell no! No sense in both of us dying.* Get him so drunk, he'd forget his suicide quest? *Doubtful*. Besides, if three beers amped Drake up to this extent, Wendell'd hate to see a full-on, bender attack.

He decided on the smartest course of action, the one he always fell back on: *inaction*.

"You know I can't stop you, Drake." Ashamed, Wendell stepped aside.

"S'what I thought." Drake huffed by him, treating him to a shoulder thump to remember him by.

"Just…be careful," Wendell said. "Don't do anything stupid or—"

The door slammed shut, Wendell's last plea lost. Like a starter pistol, it kicked Wendell's heart into overtime, his mind into overkill.

What do I do now?

With a shaky hand, he plucked his phone out. Ludicrously, he forgot the number for 911 before sensibility knocked him upside his head. Then second thoughts knocked.

Phone behind his back, he paced the small room. Ten steps one way, ten back, repeat.

If I call the cops, Big Ben will know it was me. Then he'll really be out for blood or maybe fire or making me his sex slave! Dammit! And what if Ben just really wants to talk, maybe have a few laughs, work things out like gentlemen because beneath that fur coat and clock and scary as hell image, he's a civilized man and now I'm desperate and thinking crazy nonsense that only happens in feel-good movies because the world's not made of unicorns and butterflies and—

"You want a *piece* of *me, mother—*" Outside, Drake bellowed, then abruptly stopped.

Thumps, grunts, cat-calls, groans. A crash. A trash-can rolled, loud, soft, hollow, dull… The sickening sounds of a fight, a losing one.

Wendell stumbled toward the window. He tweaked the curtain aside. Gathered back at their stoop, Big Ben's men stood in a circle. From between two men's feet, Drake's sneakers—unmistakably his thick-soled, flashy, green, athletic shoes—stuck out in a six and seven o'clock position. The men parted. Ben dominated his throne of steps, contemplating his downed opponent like a hanging judge. One man pocketed a weapon into his hoodie, a flash of metal; could've been a knife, gun, brass knuckles, who knew what, but Wendell knew damn well it could kill.

Get up, Drake, please don't be dead. God, don't let him be dead. How in hell will I ever explain this to Mom and Dad? Just get up, come back, just be slightly wounded at best, maybe learn a lesson while you're at it, but be alive and—

Drake's arms lifted, shook, criss-crossed impotently in the air. Still fighting.

Wendell cheered, just a peep, then clamped his hand over his mouth. Ducked down. Then risked another look.

Heads shook, hands waved about. For once, Wendell couldn't hear them, the conversation low and not for everyone to hear. But he had to. Carefully, slowly, he lifted the window, hoping it wouldn't produce the usual grizzly bear growl.

"…what'll we do with him, G?"

Big Ben stood, regal in his fur, and studied Drake. He kicked Drake's arm, then knelt beside him. He smiled, a gold tooth glinting from the streetlamp even at this distance. Then patted Drake's head with an unexpectedly soft touch.

"Boy's outta his head. I like that. Drag his ass inside."

The men took Ben's orders literally. One guy grabbed Drake's feet, another his hands. They dragged him up the stairs, Drake's head liquidly thumping on each step.

Over the men's laughter, Wendell heard Drake moan. Then he uttered a garbled, pointless threat, "Gonna…kill you."

The door banged shut.

Wendell's mind exploded.

Oh my God! What'm I gonna do? Just wait it out? Wait for them to kill Drake? Or worse? Jesus, what if... No, don't go there! Maybe it's time to call the cops, beyond time, the end of time to get the cops on-board! But Ben could call it self-defense. Kinda true, too. Drake did go at them first. Sorta. No, I know, I'll wait for another neighbor to call the cops. Surely one of them will! Yeah, so easy, that's what I'll do!

Hopeful, Wendell pulled back the curtain, and looked across the street. One after another, apartment lights blinked out like a faulty string of Christmas bulbs. He leaned out far, dangerously far. Next door, Big Ben's building blacked out as well. Click, click, goddamned clack. From what he could see, his building had tucked in, too.

Cowards! That's what you are, every last one! But...what's that make me? Yeah, I know I'm a chicken, first to admit it! Cluck-cluck-cluck! Hellooo! Self-preservation much? Then again, inaction never really worked out for any real chickens, the poultry kind, that is.

"*Dammit, Drake!*" Wendell paced the claustrophobic studio, the place he rarely left, the place where he had many internal conversations with himself. Most of all, the place where he felt safe.

But Drake's my brother. My responsibility. Time to man up, sack up, go over there and save his stupid ass! Yeah…that's what I'm gonna do. In a few minutes, just got to build up courage first. Just got to—

"Gah! I *so* don't want to do this!"

But I have to. Get going. Right now they could be beating the crap out of him all over again…

He rushed over to the mirror above his sink. Looked at his sweaty face, his pallid complexion. His receding hairline.

Losing my hair at the age of twenty-three! Dammit! Drake's two years older and has the hair of a gorilla! Why'd he get all the good genes! This is all his fault! Maybe I should teach him a lesson, show him he can't go around bullying everyone! Let him swing in the wind and… No! I can't do that to Drake. I mean, he used to stick up for me with my bullies. Well…when he wasn't bullying me himself. Then there was the time he…

A surge of nausea rocked him forward. He gripped the sink, ready to hurl his liquid dinner. Nothing came of it. Just his body's safety net of procrastination.

He splashed cold water on his face. Looked into the mirror one last time (and hoped it truly wasn't the *last* time). It always worked in the movies, so he coached himself through a little pep talk.

“You can *do* this. You’re gonna go over there, reason with them, apologize for Drake, make good. Maybe even snag a ‘get out of jail’ card from Big Ben for the future because he’ll like you so much. Sure. You’re gonna kill ’em with kindness. Because you’re kinder and smarter than they are. And if nothing else, you’re the fastest damn runner to ever turn tail and save his hide.”

Unlike the movies, he didn’t feel any better. His lips quivered, betraying his fear. His eyes watered, on the verge of unpacking tears. His stomach bucked again, just a how-do-you-do-I’m-still-here warning.

One last look around his studio—*goodbye, old friend*—and he left the superficial safety of his studio.

Chapter Two

7:15 P.M.

Outside Big Ben's building, Wendell inhaled deeply and prepared to dive in before his feet ran cold. While the rest of the occupants hid behind locked doors and drawn curtains, the party raged inside Big Ben's loft. Music, laughter, and shrieks involving God knows what filled the otherwise quiet street.

He opened the outer door, breezed by the announce buttons in the small foyer, and caught a ghostly glimpse of his pale, frightened image in the door's inset window. The joke of a security system required visitors to be buzzed in, but as in Wendell's building, the doors never closed properly. The inner door opened easily and he stepped into the building. Like a flame leading a moth to its inexorable death, Wendell followed the loud thumping bass and raucous laughter up three flights of stairs.

With his fist primed and ready to knock on Big Ben's metal door (*how the hell did he get a metal door?*), Wendell entertained second thoughts. And third and fourth and…

The door yanked open. Wendell gasped, hardly the suave, crush 'em with coolness entrance he'd envisioned.

Shirtless, the man gawped at Wendell, and gave

him a roller-coaster up and down appraisal. He didn't look too happy, either.

"What 'chu *want*?" Of course, Wendell recognized the squeaky, helium-affected vocalization of "Little Ben," the toady who Big Ben usually tasked with the most tedious labors.

"Ah, hi…I'm your neighbor next door and…and…" Wendell's words got away from him and his feet wanted to follow. Briefly, he considered talking to the thug on his own level, evoking a sort of tough guy image. Show him how cool Wendell could be. But as Wendell didn't have a cool bone in his body, that particularly bad idea could only end in a beating or bullets.

"Well? I ain't got all day. What 'chu want, I said?" Clearly agitated, Little Ben danced back and forth on bare feet, antsy to rejoin the party. Behind him, a woman's laughter belted out.

Wendell's testicles retracted a bit. "I…uh…" He cleared his throat, and coughed into a cupped hand to hide a dry throat click. And, man, did he hate that annoying tell-tale habit of his.

"Hey! If you got the flu or somethin', just get your ass away! I don't want no damn flu!"

"No, no…. It's not—"

"Who is it, Little Ben?" called out the host of the party.

Little Ben turned aside, and opened the door so his boss could see. With a shrug, Little Ben's narrow shoulders pinched into his cheeks. "Man, I dunno. Guy won't say nothin'."

For the first time, Wendell stared into the face of the beast. Big Ben fixed him with hungry eyes, nibbling away at what little bravery Wendell brought with him. Ben sprawled out on a luxurious, room devouring L-shaped sofa set, muscular arms draped over the back. A pretty woman sat nestled next to him, head on his shoulder. Long eyelashes blinked, a wide smile stretched. Ben's crew stood around him, apparently not invited on the furniture. In front of Ben, various drug paraphernalia and remote controls covered the coffee table.

Nothing but buddies here, Big Ben showed Wendell a gold-toothed grin. With a come-hither hand gesture, he waved Wendell inside.

As soon as Wendell cleared the doorway, the door slammed behind him. He felt the sharp report thrum into his chest. Clearly unimpressed with Wendell, Little Ben snorted, folded his arms, and walked away hugging himself.

Big Ben's impressive loft occupied the building's entire third floor, enough room to gobble at least six of Wendell's studio apartments. Although the wall paint flaked in the same manner as Wendell's abode, crime clearly paid off in buckets. Gargantuan TVs hung on three of the walls; the fourth wall, all glass, overlooked the Kansas City downtown skyline, the lights blinking and winking in a good-time way. Furniture—fresh off the truck and out of the box, price tags still attached—conquered most of the space in the vast central area.

In the far South corner, next to one of the wall-filling TVs, sat Drake in a strangely out-of-place, folding chair. One of Ben's thugs stood next to him, hand on Drake's shoulder. Out of it, Drake's head hung, his hair—wet with sweat—draped in front of him like a shroud. His wide shoulders slowly lifted and dropped, lucky guy sleeping through the drama. Beneath Drake's feet sat an industrial-sized roll of plastic.

Uh-oh.

Ben grinned, nodded in a cock-sure way, clearly enjoying Wendell's admiration of his kingdom.

Hamming it up like Easter dinner, Wendell mimed twisting a knob, put a hand to his ear, and pointed at the high-dollar music system. Shouting for armistice over rap music seemed undiplomatic. "Can you please turn it down?" he shouted.

With a sigh, Big Ben jerked his chin toward one of his lackeys. The guy didn't waste any time, bolted to the stereo, and turned it down to a dull roar.

"You lost or somethin'?" asked Ben. The woman next to him tittered, her long nails covering silicone-injected lips.

"Um, no." Warily, Wendell approached Ben. He felt naked, on display, all eyes on him. Laughter followed him through the room.

Wendell sought out his comfort zone. To his dismay, it'd packed up, gone fishing. "Hi, I'm your neighbor." Wendell stuck out his hand. Big Ben stared at it, and left him hanging. Quickly, Wendell retracted it, nervously wiped his sweaty palm on his red ankle pants, and damn, he sure wished he'd changed into something less glaring before entering Big Ben's lair.

"I don't know you. You know young-blood here, Jiggy?"

Jiggy, a thin, tall man, scratched his chin. His patchy beard grew in spots where acne war-zones hadn't sand-blasted the facial terrain. "Can't say I do, G."

"So I axc again, thc hell you doin' up in my crib?"

"Okay…" Hands up, palms open, friendly approach. "First of all, that's my brother over there. Drake." Wendell dropped his finger when he saw it wavering like a divining rod. "Second, I'd like to apologize for his—"

"Whoa, whoa, *whoa*!" Big Ben's hands went spastic. Damn big hands on wiry wrists that Wendell imagined could do a lot of damage. "What's this all about then? Why you apologizin' for your bro? Guy's a damn loud mouth, steppin' up to me and everything. You your bro's keeper?"

"I wouldn't say that, not really. But—"

"If you wouldn't say it, why you sayin' it?"

"I just—"

"Look at you, standin' there in your damn high-water red britches, comin' in here all uninvited and shit. What's up with those pants anyway? Boys, you ever seen anything like 'em?"

Jiggy gave Wendell another thorough examination. "Looks like little boy pants, G."

"They're not—"

"Speak when you're spoken to!" Big Ben jumped out of his deep sofa, came at Wendell. They'd have been nose-to-nose if Ben didn't have an entire head of height over Wendell. Wendell stared at Ben's throat.

"Sorry. Big Ben, we're getting off on the wrong foot. I—"

"Talkin' outta turn again! What'm I gonna do with you? Open to ideas." Big Ben spun in a circle, arms out, showing his cohorts how open he was.

"Waste him, G," offered the ever-helpful Jiggy.

Silence. A long, interminable, cricket-filled silence. Wendell's dry gulp carried the weight of a fat man cannonballing into a swimming pool.

Finally, Big Ben barked out seal-like laughter. Dropped a large hand around Wendell's neck and pulled him close. "Just playin' wit' cha, that's all. Just playin'. I like this guy." Still laughing, Ben swung Wendell in a dizzying circle. Although playful in action, he tightened his grip around Wendell's neck. "Sit with me. C'mon." Ben tugged. Wendell's sense of self-preservation decided to pull back. His heels dug in and he tried backing out of the stranglehold.

"Hey, hey! What's this?" Ben released Wendell. He stepped back. His golden smile dropped into a grimace. Playing hurt. Wendell almost felt sorry for the scary guy. "You come into my crib, barge in, demanding all kinds of shit and—"

"I didn't really demand anything," murmured Wendell, his inner censor wildly on the fritz.

"—now you won't even sit with me? Rude. Really damn rude."

"Damn rude, G!" Clearly the arbiter of good manners, Jiggy dug a thumbnail into his teeth, spelunking for hidden treasures.

"One thing I don't tolerate…rudeness!" Big Ben squared up (more like skyscrapered up), hands on hips, eyes glaring.

"I'm sorry, really," said Wendell. "I didn't mean—"

"Sorry, sorry, sorry, *shiiittt…* All you seem to be doin' is apologizin'. Your momma never teach you actions speak louder than words?"

"Yes." No louder than a baby bird's peep.

"Didn't hear you, youngblood!" Ben leaned in close, a hand cupped around his ear, his eyes and mouth forming expectant "O's."

"Yes. I'd love to sit with you." Wendell's smile trembled, at least a 4.9 on the Richter scale. A strange memory pestered him: his mother preaching he should use the bathroom before going places. Now more than ever, he wished he'd given his mother's lesson more credence.

Again, Big Ben dropped the threatening stance. Menacing, cloudy eyes parted for a sunnier disposition. Guy could turn on a dime. "Cool, cool!" He laughed, head up, his sonorous baritone rattling the crystals of a low-hanging chandelier. Hijacking Wendell by the shoulders, he steered him toward the sofa. The woman with the butterfly-winged eyelashes stared at him blankly, tucked her legs up beneath her. Ben relaxed back into his spot, and patted the cushion next to him. As if testing frigid waters, Wendell positioned himself on the edge of the seat, ready to swim away at the first sign of trouble.

Thumpf.

Ben landed his hand on Wendell's chest and thrust him back into the swallowing (and alarmingly cold) leather. Ben pulled the woman in close, did the same to Wendell, his arms around both their shoulders. Peas in a pod, the way lovers watched movies. Wendell sat quietly, nervously. Every time Ben patted Wendell's shoulder, his heart rocketed. Ben adjusted himself, moved his bottom back and forth, apparently digging in for a long, comfy stay. Ben's right knee jiggled, setting off edgy tremors in Wendell. His knee bounced right along with Ben's.

"Now isn't this nice?" Ben's voice slashed through the tense silence. Wendell had no idea if he could talk now or not. “I *said* ain’t this nice?”

“Yes, yes, it’s really nice,” said Wendell.

“Well, hell,” said Ben, “here I am schoolin’ you on manners and all. You know me but I still don’t know you. What they call you?”

From the corner, plastic rumpled. A groan. Then Drake’s voice, tempered by drunken slurring. “Wendy? What’re you doin’ here? Don’t tell ’em jack—”

Crack.

The thug standing next to Drake slapped him. Wendell winced, vicariously felt the sting, and gritted his teeth. Said nothing.

“Ow! *Goddammit*, let me go and we’ll *see* who—”

A punch followed. Drake’s head rocked back, then fell chin to chest. He spat. As he struggled, the folding chair bounced up and down, the front legs tap-dancing across the floor.

“Let my brother *go*, ass-hats,” yelled Drake. “*Goddammit*! He didn’t do anything! I—”

“Goddamn!” Ben’s previously friendly fingers bit deep into Wendell’s shoulder. “Tryin’ to have a friendly conversation with my man here and your bro’s really tryin’ my every nerve. Bodacious, take his ass to the back room already. Teach him some manners.”

The man called Bodacious stepped away from the pack. His beyond lazy eye wandered the room before settling somewhere in the vicinity of his boss, seeking some kind of cross-eyed visual corroboration. In no hurry, he shuffled toward Drake, his feet dusting the floor. Until he whirled, brought his leg up, and planted his foot onto Drake’s chest. The chair and Drake crashed to the floor. As Bodacious bent over to grab Drake’s legs, he exposed a plumber’s worth of crack.

Struggling, he stood, wiped his brow, and said, "Any you lazy-asses gonna help me or what?"

Another man—Big Ben appeared to have an endless supply of them—hustled over and hoisted Drake's arms up. Together, they carried Drake past the sofa. Wendell gulped. His throat tightened. As did Big Ben's grip on his shoulder.

"Don't tell 'em anything, Wendy!" screamed Drake. "You hear me? Don't give 'em nothin'! Don't—"

"Shut him the hell up!" Spittle flew from Big Ben's vocal outburst. Calmer now, he asked Wendell, "You get all the manners in your family?"

Never having really considered it until now, for a brief, crazy instant, Wendell suspected Big Ben possessed a keen insight into people. "Kinda seems that way, doesn't it?"

Ben chuckled. "So…how much did your momma hate you, anyway?"

"Ah…what do you mean?"

Big Ben sank lower, shoulder to shoulder with Wendell now. His knees pitched high, stork-leg high. "'Wendy'. Why the hell your momma give you a girl's name? Your bro, he's all Drake and shit. Cool-ass name. You got the little red-headed burger girl's name. Matter of fact, you kinda look like her, too. That Wendy girl from the restaurant, I'm talkin'."

Crap. "Oh, that. It doesn't mean anything." Wendell tried to cut through the hated nickname with a slash of nonchalance. But his voice belied his true self, trembling like latter-day Katherine Hepburn. "That's just my big brother being a dumb-ass. My name's Wendell. He used to call me 'Wendy.' You know, brother crap." Dumb eyes and a mute response met him. "You know, teasing…" Wendell felt as impotent as a neutered pet, his voice tinier than a cartoon mouse's. Yet he had to do something, be proactive, keep talking, anything to keep from screaming and running the hell out of there. "It's what brothers…what they…do…" Finally, his voice scraped the desert floor, dried out.

"Wendell. Heh. That name's 'bout as bad as Wendy. I'm gonna stick with Wendy. That all right with you, Wendy?"

Absolutely not. "Sure, whatever you say."

"I mean, really, with your red pants and red hair and all you really do look like the Wendy's girl."

"Yeah…I get that a lot."

"So, Wendy… Back to what I was sayin', your folks must hate you. They gave your bro all the looks and muscles and hair and the bad-ass name. You got the short end of the geek stick, y'know what I'm sayin'?"

As they were sitting closer than Siamese twins, Wendell had to agree. "Sure. Yeah, I guess."

"I 'spect you're one of them hipsters, Wendy. Hope that ain't the case. Me? Can't stand those beanie-wearin', coffee-swillin', kale-swallowin' dicksters. Ruinin' my neighborhood. Used to be a good neighborhood, too, 'til the hipsters started sashayin' in, tryin' to manscape the 'hood." Ben turned to fully face Wendell. He lowered his already muted voice to quiet menace. "Tell me you ain't one of them hipsters, Wendy. Your lil' boy pants kinda screams hipster to me."

If I say "yes," Big Ben will skewer me. If I say "no," then Ben'll point to my ankle pants, call me a liar, probably tear me apart and feed the scraps to Jiggy and Bodacious and... Why in the hell did I wear these stupid ankle pants? I don't even like them! They make my ass look huge! And why did I ever follow the lemming-like hipsters on their mass exodus into the K.C. Bottoms and...

Spunch. Ben's fingers squeezed the sofa leather next to Wendell's head.

"No! I'm not a hipster! I don't even *like* those guys! I hate coffee and don't even own a beanie! I'm just wearing these stupid red pants to meet girls because someone told me girls like 'em!" Worse than spewing out vomit, the lies poured forth, some of them inspired. Grace under pressure, a first in Wendell's life.

Wendell held Big Ben's gaze, the hardest thing he'd ever done. But he knew if he so much as flinched, looked away in a sideways tell, Ben would filet him.

With more solemnity and backbone than he'd drawn upon before, Wendell defiantly repeated, "I am *not* a hipster." Gregory Peck couldn't have stated it with more conviction.

Everyone in the room appeared to be collectively holding their breath, one large central nervous system plugged into mass anxiety. Big Ben's slow nod climaxed with a gentle chuckle. Relief, relaxed sighs washed over the room. Ben's posse deemed it safe to join in the laughter. So did Wendell.

"Why you laughin', Wendy?" asked Ben, suddenly serious. "You ain't outta the woods yet. So…if you ain't a hipster. What are you?"

"Me? I'm just Wendell Worthy, a—"

"Wendy Worthy? Jaysus Christ! What, you some kinda rich guy slummin' it or somethin'?"

"No, no, no. Nothing like that."

"Then what *are* you?"

Out of the frying pan and into the fire. How should I answer the question? Should I say I'm—

"Goddammit, Wendy!" Another punch to the much-tortured sofa, this time barely missing Wendell's head. "This ain't brain surgery! Who are you? Whaddaya do? Christ! Kids today!"

Although Wendell suspected Ben was a couple of years younger than himself, he let it pass. "Oh, um…I'm a writer." The truth, but it could go either way. He didn't suspect Ben and company patronized the KCMO library.

Thoughtful, Ben leaned back, finger massaging his lower lip. "Huh. A writer. You mean books and shit?"

"Well, yeah. I mean I'm trying to."

"Trying to? The hell's that mean? You a writer or ain't you?"

"Yes, I'm a—"

"What you write? Bedazzle us with some writing you wrote." Ben threw out sparkly fingers; let them float down to his lap.

Wendell rubbed the back of his head. Kind of warm and sweaty back there from Ben's constant kneading, grabbing and pinching. Plus, he needed time, glad to buy time, someone give him a damn credit card for time. "Well, it's kinda complicated to explain—"

Ben's eyes narrowed. "Wendy, you talkin' down to me? You think I'm too dumb to read? That what you doin'?"

"No! Of course not! I—"

Ben dropped a finger over Wendell's lips. "Shhhh. Shh, shh, shh, Wendy. Big Ben's talkin'." Gently, he patted the side of Wendell's face, a beloved lap dog. "I get the feelin' you think you're better than me. And that just ain't cool. It just ain't. 'Specially when you come in here actin' all high-falutin', Mr. Big-Time, College Boy, Writer, In-too-lectu-all," —finger quotes went up like danger signs— "and everything. Now, either you a writer or you ain't. You understand me?" This time the slap didn't land so gently. "You get me, Wendy?" Wendell nodded, too afraid to speak. Afraid of the crackling voice that he knew would come out. More afraid of the crackling sound his bones would produce beneath Ben's fists. "Good girl. Now…let's talk literature."

Wendell's voice ground out like a car's engine succumbing to a dying battery. "The book I'm working on is—"

"What's the name of it?"

"Ah…um…" Wendell had the title, all right. Knew it well, had it picked out before he'd even left middle school. Knew it'd be the book title that'd launch his brilliant literary career. Now everything he thought he knew came back on him as sure as if he'd spat into the wind. Suddenly in this loft, sitting on this sofa, his book title sounded incredibly trite and stupid. But he couldn't create a valid-sounding, fake title holder. Not spur of the moment, not under pressure. Not before the knives and guns and weapons of minor destruction came out. He shut his eyes, and blurted out, "*A Pocketful of Heart*!"

"*A Pocketful…* What the hell kinda book name is *that*?" Ben played up to his cronies like a stand-up comic, hand out in a "You believe this?" manner. "You guys hear that? *A Pocketful of Heart*! Sounds kinda gay to me!" On a tear, Big Ben lolled around on the sofa. "What's this book of yours about, Wendy? Love story? Romance for lil' ol' ladies?"

Wendell weighed his literary integrity against his survival chances. Didn't take a Vegas odds-maker to figure out which way he'd lean. He rushed his words out quickly, hoping no one would latch on. "It's a book about a writer who moves to Kansas City to live life and—"

"Wait, wait a minute, hol' on a sec!" Ben crossed his wrists, a personal foul. "You tellin' me you're writing a book about a guy who's writing a book?"

"Um, kind of. But it's about more than that. It's a coming of—"

"Wendy, this sounds dumb as hell. So, you tellin' me people supposed to get all excited and jump up and down 'bout a book about a guy sittin' at a typewriter and shit? Any action? Guys cappin' one another? Like real life?"

"Ah, no…it's not that kind of book. But there's—"

"'Not that kinda book'. What's that supposed to mean? You—what's the word I'm lookin' for—you disparagin' me or somethin'? Lookin' down your college boy nose at me? At my lifestyle? My life ain't good enough to be in a book?"

Jesus, here we go again. "Not at all, Big Ben. I have the utmost respect for you and your lifestyle." *And my life.* "I don't… I don't think I could possibly do your lifestyle justice. Give it the writing it deserves, right? I mean…really, what do I know about your…um, lifestyle?" Wendell tried on what he thought might be a friendly lawyer's look, all smiles and lies. "I'm just not fit to write about your life. It's…it's bigger than life."

To show how big, Wendell's hands went wide.

Satisfied, Ben settled back. He looked at the woman next to him, apparently seeking her counsel. She twirled her hair, smiled, all lips, no teeth: *blessed approval*. "Got it, got it," said Ben. "Maybe we'll have a sit-down. I'll tell you 'bout my life. You can immortalize me. Sound good, Wendy?"

No. If I get out of this, I'm moving tomorrow. "Sounds like a great idea, Big Ben. Maybe next week, I'll, um, have my lawyer draw up a contract and—"

"What? You don't trust me?" His hands dug beneath his pits, hissy-fitting. "What? My word ain't good enough for you? Mr. Ivy League Tower and all? My word is solid. Big Ben don't need no goddamn contracts. Ain't that right, Jiggy?"

"Word, G."

"Just looking after your best interests, Big Ben, that's all." More confident, Wendell thought his lawyer's wing-tipped shoes slipped on quite nicely. After all, when you're pleading for your life, it's a natural. "I want to make sure you get the best financial deal out of it."

Ben's eyebrows knit together. His business look. "Fine, then, that's what it takes. But I ain't saddlin' up with no loser. You makin' good bank on your book?"

Oh, boy. Worse than my family dinners. "Well…that's not exactly how the publishing industry works. First, I need to finish the book. Then—"

"Whoa! You ain't even finished the book?"

"No. Not yet." Although used to the shame by now, all the smirks and sideways glances still hurt when Wendell told people about the struggling part of the literary journey. Few understood nothing but the money. He certainly didn't expect to get the same derision from a street thug, sitting kissing distance from him on his blood-bought sofa set. "Sometimes it takes an artist a long time to—"

"Now you're an artist. First, you're a writer, then an artist. How you livin'?"

"Sorry?"

"What you doin' to pay the bills? Bring home the bacon? Can't do it on pipe-dreams, am I right?"

"Right as rain, G," said Ben's one-man Greek chorus, Jiggy.

"So what do you do, Wendy?"

"Um…well… Temporarily, 'til I sell my book, I'm supplementing my income waiting tables down at the Jaybird Bistro." *Boom*! Thunder. Wendell waited for the inevitable rain.

"Shiiiit," said Ben, now leaning forward, hands hung between his knees. "You ain't no writer. Certainly ain't no ar-teeste! You're a waiter."

Wendell couldn't help himself, flung back finger-quotes. "I'm only a 'waiter' for *now*. Until my book sells. And it will."

"Nope. Nothin' but a damn waiter. Am I right or what?"

"Nailed it on the head, G."

"You know somethin' Wendy? I'm kinda gettin' bored with your ass now. Why'm I wastin' time with a waiter? You guys a dime a dozen. And my time is golden." He tapped his chest clock as irrefutable truth. "Tell me somethin' interestin' 'bout yourself. 'Fore I take out the trash."

And, of course, by "taking out the trash," Wendell had no doubt what Ben meant.

Yet Ben's proposition presented a huge challenge for Wendell. Wendell—and by extension, practically everyone he knew—didn't find himself very interesting. Always a shadow person, skulking behind others, riding the rails of anonymity.

Then it hit Wendell, his one full-fledged accomplishment. Born out of the need to survive, something he could definitely own. "I can run," he said. "I can run *fast*."

The spotlight closed in on Wendell, hot and claustrophobic. Now, of course, all he wanted to do was slink back behind the curtain, and hide out until the coast was clear. Instead, he repeated himself, this time stronger and louder. "I can run really, *really* fast."

"That so?" Ben shoved his long-lashed bimbo aside, the more attention to lavish on Wendell. "Now *that's* interestin'."

"I think so," added Wendell.

"No one axed you, Wendy. But you, like, gold medal fast or somethin'?"

"Nothing like that. I just…learned how to run fast."

"You *learned*? How in hell you do that? You either got it or you don't. You know, the way God made ya." He crossed himself, lifted the clock from his chest, kissed it, although Wendell hardly saw the relevance. "So, how you learn?"

"Long story. Back in high school, I—"

"I say, how you learn, Wendy?"

Apparently, Ben didn't appreciate long stories, so Wendell cut to the chase. "In high school, I was bullied. I learned to run fast. Really fast. Taught myself. Didn't stop until I could do it, faster than anyone." He shrugged, even though he actually took pride in his achievement.

“Not everybody can be a champion, takes all kinds.” Ben thumped his admittedly impressive chest, one rivaling Drake’s. He stood, paced the length of the sofa. “Damn, you give me a good idea. You like games, Wendy?”

“Um, depends…”

“Listen to this guy, thinks we’re in a democracy.” Ben stopped in front of Wendell. Arms open and ready for a hug, Ben leaned over. Then he jerked Wendell to his feet. No sweat, no exertion, just two hands beneath Wendell’s pits and up he flew.

“Tell you what, Wendy,” said Ben, “I’m hungry.”

“Ah…I’m not much of a cook.”

“Course not! Cookin’s a woman’s job! Unless you part girl. You part girl, Wendy? That’d explain it all. You got the name for it.”

“No, I’m not part girl. I just said—”

Smek. The slap stunned Wendell, stung like a sunburn. Given Wendell’s complexion, he knew the mark shone as bright as a red barn on a sunny day.

“Never interrupt me, Wendy! Verdict’s still out whether you part girl or not. Ain’t that right?”

“Hung jury, G.” Jiggy’s response drew laughter.

“But we’re gonna find out. You want your loudmouth, dumb-ass bro back in one piece?”

Ben shook him by his shirt collar, shook out Wendell’s answer. “Yes. Please?”

“Dunno why you think he’s the shit, but I’m a fair man. Reasonable as Judge Judy. Tell you what I’m gonna do. I’m hungry. Got a real hankerin’ for some of Marion’s Louisiana chili. Ever been to Marion’s?”

“Can’t say I have.”

"You either been there or not. None of this 'can't say I have' crap." His high-pitched imitation of Wendell didn't ring true, not to Wendell's ears. "Anyway, it's the best damn chili in Kansas City! Word. You know where *Marion's Eats and Drinks* is, Wendy?"

Again, a slow head shake, not too deliberate, not too fast.

"It's down at 12th and Brooklyn. Kinda where Vine Street used to be, some park there now. You bring me some Marion's chili by… Let's see. It's…" He lifted the clock from his chest, squinted, puzzled over upside down time. "It's about eight fifteen now. You get it to me in two hours, I'll cut your bro loose. Then we're even."

Inside, Wendell felt a huge smile birthing, one that threatened to explode. He'd gotten off easy. No sweat. He could drive round-trip to Marion's in fifteen minutes and that's taking his time. Easy-peasy. No matter how hard Wendell tried to temper a victory grin, it won its way out.

"Sounds like a fair deal. Thanks." As soon as Wendell stuck his hand out again, he wished he hadn't. Something seemed off. Ben's grin overwhelmed Wendell's by sheer razzle-dazzle and a peculiar "I-know-something-you-don't-know" gleam in his eye.

"Hold up," said Big Ben. "We ain't done yet. There's some rules to our game and all."

"Rules…"

"What I said. Gimme your car keys." For once, Ben offered his hand to Wendell.

"What?" As if to protect his keys, Wendell shoved his hands in his pockets. True, his car was a jacked-up

Celica, no better than a glorified skate board, but it was the only transportation he had. The rough edges of the car key raked across his finger. For a panic-driven second, he considered forcing the keys between his clenched fingers and jabbing his way out. Then common sense caged his inner wolverine.

"Your keys, Wendy! Gimme your goddamn keys! I know I don't stutter!"

Hesitantly, Wendell handed them over. Part of Wendell—the naïve part that still believed in the goodness of humanity—thought surely there'd be a last-minute reprieve. A "just kidding" moment for the benefit of Ben's pals. But Ben snatched them away, and studied them.

"What? Japanese?"

"A, um, Celica."

"Some American you are, Wendy. Piece of crap car."

"Fine. So I'll take an Uber or—"

"You don't get it, dawg! This a game we playin'. With any games, there gots to be challenges. None of that Uber crap. Now, gimme your wallet."

"*What*? My wallet? How'm I supposed… How am I gonna…" A slow-burn built on Big Ben's face. Wendell quit arguing, retreated, and whipped out his wallet. "Here. Take it. No problem. Part of the challenge—"

Impossibly fast, Ben knocked the wallet from Wendell's hand. It flew through the air. Wendell watched it—one of those odd, slow motion, end over end trajectories that movies immortalized—and suddenly his feet left the ground as well. Ben kicked out Wendell's legs, grabbed his shirt front and slammed him to the floor. Out of breath and stunned, Wendell looked up at the towering figure of Big Ben. Ben finalized his conquest by planting his sneaker on top of Wendell's chest.

"You just don't get what's what, Wendy." Ben's breathing regulated to a passably human sound. Triumphant, he raised his arms, a modern day gladiator in the arena of his loft. "I got somethin' you want. You ain't got jack to offer me." He knelt down, his knee pressing into Wendell's ribcage. "So quit givin' me shit and play the game." He stood, his foot still on Wendell's chest. Finally, he lifted it.

Cautiously, Wendell said, "Okay, I understand. I've got two hours to get to Marion's, get your chili and get back in time. I can't drive. Fine. I can't take a cab or call an Uber. I get it. But can I at least have my money for the chili?"

"What'd I say? My rules. Play 'em or you never get your bro back."

Another challenge, one he'd worry about later. Frankly, he just wanted to get the hell out of there. "Fine. How far is Marion's?"

"I look like a GPS to you?"

"No."

"Jiggy, how far's Marion's?"

"'Bout…three miles straight up 12th," said Jiggy.

With the aid of his fingers, his eyes shut, Big Ben did some quick computations. "Even if you walked it, that's what…twenty minutes a mile. My gramma could make it there and back in two hours and that's using her damn walker. You said you could run fast. Let's see you do it. More than fair."

It wasn't, not by a long-shot, but he couldn't win,

not with this jury.

"Get your ass off the floor, Wendy. Downright undignified lookin'."

"Kinda trashy-lookin', G," said Jiggy.

Wendell crawled to his knees, testing the strength of his sailor's legs before standing.

"More rules, fellas, I want more rules." Hands folded behind his back, Ben strut in front of his gang like a college professor on a roll.

Bodacious offered, "Take his phone."

"Good call, B." Again, Ben held out his hand and Wendell complied. "Now, I just got me a killer idea, helluva idea. Wendy, take off your clothes."

Wendell's stomach sunk. His testicles retracted even further, settling somewhere in his gut, raising a swell of nausea. His ears burned. Heat—clammy in the air and heavy—threatened to drop him. He wanted to doubt what he'd heard, but his traitorous brain blasted him with the truth.

"I said take off your goddamn *clothes*!"

A test, plain and simple, that's all. Big Ben likes to play games, respects guys who man up even against the scariest odds. Surely he doesn't want me to take my clothes off. Of course he doesn't!

"Come on," Wendell eked out. "I can't go anywhere without my clothes. You're kidding, right?" Wendell followed with a half-hearted conspiratorial wink and disarming grin.

Silence dropped over the room, more reverently hushed than a funeral parlor. Some of the men looked askance, at their shoes, anywhere but at Wendell. Hardly an encouraging sign.

Two giant steps—the only kind Ben took—and he

grabbed Wendell. With a scream, he lifted Wendell, pitched him over the coffee table and onto the sofa. Wendell's head bounced off the woman's lap. She afforded him a fleeting glance, quietly got up and walked toward the back where they'd taken Drake.

Ben raged. Saliva flew from his mouth. "*What* in our goddamn interaction tonight makes you *think* I'm *kidding*?" He reached down, picked Wendell up by the collar of his now outstretched shirt and banged him against the wall. A picture of Jesus slid down behind Wendell, cracked into the wall. "*When're* you gonna start takin' me *seriously*? What's it gonna *take*?"

Big Ben yanked him off the sofa. Like a practiced dancer, he twirled Wendell around, jacked Wendell's arm up behind him, and cradled Wendell's back to his chest. They swayed together, Ben's chin resting on top of Wendell's head. With Ben leading, scariest slow dance ever. "Guess I'm gonna have to prove how serious I am." The menacing whisper blew hot against Wendell's ear. In a louder voice, Ben ordered, "Get Napoleon in here!"

A stampede of Big Ben's underlings tromped toward the mysterious back room. Soon, a voice—scared and pleading and all too understandable—rose above the excitement of the others.

"C'mon, BB, gimme a break, man. We buddies, we go back. I was gonna pay it back. You know I'm good for it, G. Didn't mean nothin', just playin'…"

From the hallway, the men dragged Napoleon toward the corner Drake had occupied earlier. Roughly, they forced him down into the folding chair. His feet kicked. Plastic rumpled beneath him.

"Wanna see how I kid around, Wendy? C'mon, up

close and personal. Ring-side seat." Ben caught Wendell's neck in the crutch of his arm. Rather than being dragged, Wendell half ran, head down, to keep up with Ben. His feet lagged behind Ben's wide stride. The tips of his sneakers caught on the hardwood floor, squeaking toward the corner of torture. He clung onto Ben's arm so as not to choke.

One mighty shove and Wendell met the floor, close to Napoleon's feet. Held firmly in place by two of Ben's men, Napoleon put up a good fight, unaware of Wendell's presence. Other things on his mind.

"C'mon, now, BB, you know me. We're brothers! I wasn't gonna cheat you!" Napoleon's words dissolved into soup. His eyes narrowed. His nose sat crooked, a ski-jump of torn mucilage. Plump, beaten lips gave the departed bimbo stiff competition. Tears mingled with blood, his face a swampland of grief.

"Don't know any such thing, Nap," said Big Ben. "Jiggy, hit the tunes. Play it loud and make it good."

Music exploded. Wendell's heart rattled against its ribcage prison. His bowels danced, twirled in his body's blender.

Big Ben felt the music, too. His eyes closed. Around Napoleon he danced, smooth and nimble, almost a ritualistic dance. He reached behind him, pulled out a gun—the gun Wendell just knew would materialize sooner than later—brought it up in one swift move. Pulled the trigger.

The hammering bass obscured the blast. But the results spattered Wendell's face. He couldn't hear his screams above the music. Nothing but the incessant *thump, thump, thump* of the music. Perfectly complementing his heart's manic beat.

Wendell scrabbled back, madly clawing at his hair, wiping his face with his shirt. Propelled by screams, he kept moving, a crab sliding backward across the floor, unable to stop. The coffee table poked him in the back.

At the opposite end of the room, the men stood around the remains of Napoleon's body. Laughing. Big Ben lording it over his minions, a good time had by all.

Wendell leaned over, and threw up. Did it again.

The music stopped.

The sudden death of sound jarred Wendell. He held his breath. Waited for the next bullet to smash his skull to bits.

The room swayed, a crazy merry-go-round Wendell wanted to jump off of if he could only find the mental footing.

A squeaky voice, Little Ben, called out, "We got trouble, G!" He peered out the small panel set into the metal door. "Five-Oh!"

"Well, shit," said Big Ben. "Shoulda' listened to my horoscope this morning."

Chapter Three

8:30 P.M.

“Is it Bookes?” asked Big Ben. “Big ol’ bad Dayton Bookes?”

Little Ben nodded.

“All right, clean this mess up lightning time.” Big Ben wagged his gun toward Napoleon’s body. “Wrap him up and get him in back.”

Little Ben and Jiggy moved fast, a well-synchronized team. Plenty of practice, no doubt. They rolled Napoleon up in the plastic and carried him down the hall. Little Ben, not up to the physical demands, dropped the legs. An ink-blot of dark blood squirted onto the floor.

“Goddamn, man, watch what you’re doin’!” Jiggy dropped the corpse’s arms, and thrust his fists onto his hips.

“Guy weighs a ton,” said Little Ben.

Calmly, Big Ben shook his head. Grinned as if his children had just said the cutest darn thing.

Wendell, on the other hand, didn’t find anything cute about what he’d just witnessed. His world appeared to have stopped. Everything revolved at a slower pace as he struggled to catch up, hook some solid reality connections. He wondered why the cop at the front door was patiently waiting. Hoped like hell he'd charge in like the cavalry. The only chance for Wendell and Drake's survival.

Twin Big Bens hovered over Wendell, the images wavering, finally soldering into one man. "Go on, get your ass up." His voice echoed, still the vocal equivalent of two men. "You say anything, Wendy, you and your bro ain't gonna live to see tomorrow."

Wendell put his hands on the floor, forced himself to his knees. Something warm and wet slipped down his cheek, plopped to the floor. A tear of Napoleon's blood.

"Gah!" Frantic, Wendell scrubbed at his face, walking the tightrope of hysteria.

A towel landed in front of him. "Clean up. Your momma never teach you about hygiene?" Ben tapped his foot, disgusted, impatient.

Wendell grabbed the towel, clung to it like a childhood teddy bear. He wiped his face, his neck, any exposed skin. Brushed his shirt. Without glancing at the towel—he couldn't bear seeing what had been on him; his imagination already more than overcompensated—he pitched it behind the sofa. As he tried to get up again, he stumbled back over the coffee table.

"Goddammit!" Big Ben snagged Wendell's wrist and hauled him to his feet. "Now sit your ass down on the sofa! Remember, you signin' both your death warrants, you do anything cute." His finger went to his lips: *dead men tell no tales*.

Message received. Wendell nodded, best way to communicate. Couldn't talk if he'd wanted to.

One last look around, Big Ben declared everything good and swirled his hand in the air. Showtime. "All right, let Bookes in." He collapsed onto the sofa, his leg pressing into Wendells'. Wendell smelled his own fear—hoped it wasn't the last of Napoleon lingering—a sort of sour, stale desperation.

One of Ben's men opened the door, and stood aside.

A bear of a man swept in, hyperventilating as if he'd just climbed the three flights of stairs at a rush. His suit appeared too small around his midsection, too large in other places. He pulled his pants up by the belt loops, obsessively so. His formidable gut provided staunch opposition. Sweat darkened the underarms of his jacket. A stubby finger jabbed at Big Ben as he approached the sofa. The cop knew how to make an entrance. And he didn't look happy.

"You keep me waitin'? Me? I'll kick your ass from here to Iowa you do that again, Benji!"

"Yo, chill, Bookes! Couldn't hear you over the music. And don't call me Benji! Ain't my name!" Ben offered him an award-caliber smile, full of gold. Wendell folded into himself, trying to present as small a visual object as possible. Hands clasped together, he hung them between trembling knees.

Bookes knocked his head back, and laughed at the ceiling. "Hell it ain't. You're Benjamin Landers, born the way your poor momma unleashed you onto the world. And I ain't about to call you some bullshit, wanna-be, gangsta name. 'Big Ben' my ass…*Benji.*"

Wendell sensed Big Ben's cool heating up. Body heat seemed to roll off him in waves. He sat straighter, stiff and tense, his knee bone digging into Wendell's. Ready to pounce like a tiger. "Yeah, what's up with *your* name, Bookes? Dayton Bookes. Fssh…" Ben slashed a dismissive hand, then grinned. "Sounds like some kinda bookstore for lil' ol' ladies."

"Punk-ass, makin' fun of my name? *Mine*?" Bookes thumped his chest, sounding like a large, ripe watermelon. Putting two and two together, Wendell figured they'd been battling for king of the jungle status for some time. "I'm your goddamn parole officer! You best remember that. And from now on, you address me as sir, Officer Bookes, or commander-in-chief 'cause I can take you down like that." His fingers snapped with a startling pop. "I eat punks like you for breakfast, hungry for more at lunch." He scratched at his goatee, then embarked upon a round-the-world belt loop tugging trip of his pants. "Now how 'bout tellin' me why it took you so damn long to open the door." Bookes looked around, squinted, ducked his head as if using x-ray vision to find Ben's dirty, hidden secrets. Then his gaze finally locked onto Wendell. Always intimidated by authority, Wendell turned away. An experienced cop would surely see the fear in his eyes.

"And what the hell's *he* doin' here, Benji? He don't look like your usual pals."

Wendell studied his hands as if they were the most interesting thing in the loft. But, out of the corner of his eye, he saw Bookes' outstretched arm, his judgmental finger stuck out, ready to pass judgment on Wendell.

"This's my boy, Wendy. We just chillin', that's all," said Ben.

"*Wendy*. Huh. Like the girl from the burger place?" asked Bookes.

Still looking at his hands, Wendell sighed, said, "Well, not really. My name's Wendell and—"

"Whaddaya doin' here?" Bookes stepped closer. Wendell looked up, eye level with Bookes' belly. The cop's shirt pulled at the buttons.

“Tole you we just chillin’,” said Ben.

“I’m askin’ Strawberry here, Benji. Let him talk.”

Of course, Wendell wanted to jump up, scream the truth, proudly proclaim he wasn’t a “strawberry.” But he also knew Drake would die. Ben and his cronies lacked any moral compass, probably would love to go down in a hailstorm of bullets. And take everyone they could with them. Besides, Wendell didn’t know if he could trust the large cop. Something about Bookes’ relationship with Ben seemed odd.

But he had to say something to Bookes. “Um, yeah…we’re just chilling. Like Big Ben said.” Ben dropped an arm around Wendell’s shoulders. Wendell flinched, hopefully not noticeable.

“Yep, just two guys chillin’ on the sofa, Bookes.”

“Bullshit.” Hands in his pockets, his suit jacket swept back, Bookes looked at the two of them in turn. “What you here for, really? You’re just a little strawberry. Scared of your own shadow, a red-headed groundhog. You lookin’ to score some of Benji’s blow? That why you’re here, Strawberry?”

“Now you hurt my feelings, Bookes,” said Ben. “You know I don’t dabble in drugs. That’s—whaddaya call it?—uncouth, that’s what drugs are. I’m one couth sumbitch.”

“’Bout as couth as my mother-in-law. I know you’re dirty. Got your little dirty fingers into every pie you can find. Playin’ big man.”

“Why *are* you here, Bookes? You’re crushin’ my good times.” Ben crossed his legs, exposed a bracelet wrapped around his ankle, the kind parole officers bestow upon their new BFF’s. He tapped it. “You know the GPS don’t lie. I ain’t left this general vicinity. Been a good boy."

Bookes gave his right cheek a little wet-sounding massage, finished at his double chin. His gaze never left the two sofa prisoners. "I don't like you, Benji. You're nothin' but a low-life, scumbag, murdering, drug dealin' asshole. One of these days you're gonna screw up. That's why I'm here. Keepin' hope alive. And when you screw up, I'll be there to slap your ass into Leavenworth for life."

"This's soundin' real close to police harassment. You keep up on current affairs, Bookes?"

"No, I'm too busy chasin' your worthless, lyin' ass around."

"You know where to find me." Again, Ben tapped his ankle. Smiled.

For all their posing and bickering, the ensuing silence seemed much worse. Wendell looked down at his hands again; just couldn't seem to get enough of them tonight. Then he noticed it: a splotch of blood on his pants leg. He shuffled his hand over the spot. Almost added a nonchalant hum, but he'd already had enough overkill tonight.

In lieu of parting words, Bookes pointed twin fingers at his eyes, turned them around on Ben, then Wendell. He stormed toward the door, flung it open, and left.

Torn between relief and anxiety, Wendell didn't move. Glued to the sofa, he closed his eyes, sought out peace of mind. Instead, a chaotic slide-show of the earlier bloodbath played out on his mind's screen.

"Damn Bookes." Ben turned to face Wendell. "Stupid cop's always bustin' my balls. Why you 'spose that is, Wendy?"

Not desiring to end up wrapped in plastic like Napoleon, Wendell carefully composed the safest possible answer. “Some people…ah…they’re just mad at the world. You know…they take it out on others. Because they’re jealous.” Basically repeating what the ineffective high school counselors had told Wendell about bullies.

Ben hovered over Wendell like a drone. At long last, Ben’s lips pulled back, a gold tooth a shiny, optimistic exclamation point.

“Damn, Wendy, you’re right! Some people got no class, no psychiatric repose.”

Surprised, Wendell smiled too. Bad mistake.

“Somethin’ funny, Wendy?” Ben stood, clapped his hands as if wiping away the last of Napoleon, then suddenly dropped them on Wendell’s shirt lapels. Yanked him up. “We got unfinished business. Take off your clothes.” Ben shoved Wendell toward the center of the room. Wendell’s arms flapped, an awkward attempt to maintain balance.

“Go on, Wendy, take ’em off!”

Wendell closed his eyes. Slowly, he unbuttoned his shirt.

Jesus, God, I’m gonna die. I’m gonna die naked too. Naked, cold, and alone. I’ll never get my masterpiece written, I’ll never—

“Faster, dammit, I’m hungry!”

“That’s right, G. Damn hungry.” Jiggy and Little Ben had reentered the main room. Apparently, they’d wrapped their work up quickly, not wanting to miss the floor show.

Wendell’s shirt slipped off, dropped to the floor. He hesitated. Stalled for time as he fiddled with his belt.

The circle of men grew impatient as Wendell searched their eyes, waiting—praying—for one of them to come to his senses and proclaim the joke had gone on long enough. Then again, they were a sadistically fun-loving bunch.

Suddenly Ben's gun appeared in his hand, hastening Wendell's striptease.

Embarrassed by the pasty color of his skin—his only two options: alabaster white or fire hydrant red—Wendell closed his eyes again. He had to shimmy out of his red ankle pants, form-fitting as a leather glove. Jiggy giggled. Wendell kicked off his shoes, then kicked the damned pants—*never again!* —across the room.

In his socks and underwear, Wendell dared to be defiant. He held out his hands, show-biz style: *Ta daaa! That's all, folks! No more!* Arms folded, he let his body language express his humiliation had ended. Honestly, he couldn't cite where this sudden act of defiance came from, particularly when faced with a psycho drug dealer packing a loaded gun. It surprised him more than anyone. But damned if he'd go "full monty" for their amusement. In a way, he felt bolstered by his new courage, a runner's second wind pumping iron into his veins.

Honestly, he expected a beating, at least more intimidation. Instead, led by Ben, his audience howled with laughter.

"Jesus, Wendy! Tighty-whities! Your momma dress you this mornin' or what?" Doubled over—*way* over the top—Big Ben clutched his gut, the other hand dangerously waving his gun around.

"Good one, G," said Jiggy. "Tighty-whities."

Frankly, Wendell'd forgotten he'd put them on this morning. It's not like he had a drawer full of stupid, white briefs at his apartment, nothing like that. Usually he wore more manly undergarments—boxers and boxer briefs in shades of dark, sexy colors—in hopes of impressing the ladies with his classy taste and machismo: the perfect metrosexual.

But Big Ben had caught him on Laundry Day Eve.

Manly hardly defined how Wendell felt now. His tormenters pointed, laughed, catcalled, whistled, and clucked like chickens. The underwear seemed to be shrinking, growing even tighter, threatening to strangle his penis and pop his testicles like bubble wrap. Childish move or not, he covered himself with both hands and felt even smaller for the infantile maneuver. His limp smile worsened matters.

The crowd's roar settled to a few mirthless-sounding chuckles, always one idiot trying to keep the party going.

"Goddamn, Wendy, I think I'm gonna throw up." This coming from the psycho who nonchalantly just blew a man's brains out. Ben covered his mouth, his gun cocked up beneath his nose. "But I got a rock-solid constitution."

"Rock solid, G."

Wendell made a silent vow: *If I get out of this alive, I'm gonna bitch-slap the hell out of Jiggy.*

"Now get those tighty-whities off," said Ben.

With one thumb inside the elastic, Wendell pulled it out. Then let it snap back. At this point, death by gunshot would be almost better than suffering more humiliation. The revolution had begun. Wendell moved slowly, crossed his arms again. Even though his physique wasn't up to par—David against Goliath, minus the slingshot—he stood strong.

"No," he declared.

Ben's jaw dropped. Dumbfounded, he looked at his sycophant collective. They remained quiet. So quiet, Wendell imagined he heard blood dripping in the back room.

"*What'd* you say?"

Wendell spread his legs, squared them up with his shoulders. Admittedly, he didn't have far to move, but pride made it feel like a mile. "I said, 'no.'"

Ben moved in. He lifted his gun, the barrel lined up with the bridge of Wendell's nose. "I'll be goddamned, Wendy. I really thought your bro got all the balls in the family." The gun lowered, wagged at his genitals, moved back up. "You don't wanna piss me off. You tryin' to do that?"

"No." Inwardly, Wendell cringed. When he opened his mouth, it popped dryly. But he was all in now. "I'm not trying to piss you off. But I'm *not* taking off my underwear."

The gun didn't move, neither did its owner. "I gave you an order." Ben's tone remained calm, his gun sure as hell stable in his hand. But Wendell thought he detected curiosity in Ben, possibly befuddlement. Tread carefully. *Understatement.*

"You want your chili, right?" said Wendell, going for it. "No way it's gonna happen if I'm naked. No way." Turn it around, highlight the promise. Maybe his college marketing courses weren't a complete wash-out after all.

"Boy's gotta point," said Ben.

"Seems like he's gotta point, G," said Jiggy.

The gun went down. Ben's smile rose. "Well, I'm fair. Fair as hell." Wendell thought arguing the point would just bring the gun back up again. "I'm suave and couth and fair as hell, Wendy. Get your shoes back on."

As Wendell dropped to the floor, Ben dug back into the sofa.

"Got me yet another idea. Wendy, you're really inspirin' me tonight." Ben's leg popped up onto the coffee table. He pulled up his sweat pants leg, the one with the ankle monitor. "Dakeem! Do your stuff."

Tall and wiry, Dakeem shuffled over, bent at the waist as if he had back issues. A toothpick dangled precariously from his lower lip, absolutely defying gravity. Beside his boss, he lowered to his knees and brought out a paper sack.

His butt cold on the hard-wood floor, Wendell tied his shoes as he kept a wary eye on the men. Dread filled him at the thought of a new circle of Hell opening up.

"Dakeem here's a real Mona Lisa with the electronics." Ben patted Dakeem's head. "Go on, Dakeem, tell him how it is."

Although Big Ben's metaphor made no sense whatsoever, Wendell noticed a similarity in the man's barely existent, noncommittal smile to the famous painting.

"I can do it all," Dakeem said.

"Dakeem don't like to talk too much," continued Ben. "But that's okay. I could use more like him."

From Wendell's disadvantaged viewpoint, it appeared Dakeem had pulled out wire cutters and a length of wire from his bag.

"Dakeem don't need to gab to do what he does," said Ben. "This ain't my first time bein' on house arrest, Wendy. Probably not the last." A round of subtle chuckles. "Dakeem here keeps me on the fast and free side of things. Ain't that right, Dakeem?"

"That's right."

"My boy finds the wires that complete the circuit on the monitor. He loops another wire around them, snips between 'em, and bang, circuit remains working, transmittin' the signal. And I'm good to go. That about right, Dakeem?"

Dakeem shrugged. "That's about right." He held up the still lit device, handed it to his leader.

Ben tossed it up, caught it. "You got scrawny chicken legs, Wendy," he said.

"Um, thanks?"

Ben nodded. "You're gonna wear my monitor."

Yep. This gets worse and worse.

"Sounds like a fun idea, Big Ben. But your parole officer…Bookes…is gonna track the GPS and come after me. He'll wonder why *I'm* wearing it and not you! He'll—"

"Goddamn, Wendy, live a little! Have fun for once!"

While Wendell never considered the way his humdrum life had been going lately very much fun, it felt like a barrelful of monkeys compared to tonight. "I still don't think—"

"I axe you to think?"

Fully schooled, Wendell shook his head.

"That's right. Look here, if I get to jack with Bookes a bit, win-win. It's up to you to stay a step ahead of him. 'Cause I ain't getting implicated in nothin'. If Bookes comes sniffin' round here, I'm tellin' him *you* lifted the monitor off me." Ben wiggled his newly freed leg, dropped it to the floor, and strolled toward Wendell. “Try it on.”

Much too large, the bracelet slipped easily over Wendell’s shoe. He moved it up until it stuck above his knee like a garter. He shook his head. “I can barely walk, let alone run with this on.”

“Man, I don’t care where you put it! Stick it in your tighty-whities. Kinda looks like you need a lil’ somethin’-somethin’ down there anyway.”

“Good one, G!”

“I’ll figure it out.” Wendell moved the bracelet to his arm, nudged it up until it remained fairly secure. It might stay, probably not. Better just to hold it.

“And since I wanna make sure you play by the rules, we’re gonna track you too. We can do that, right, Dakeem?”

“That’s right.”

“Maybe I even send out some of my boys to keep you on your toes. All right! We done! Game time!” Ben picked up his clock, looked at it. “Damn, son, how’d it get to be this late already? Nine-twenty in the P.M.!” He rubbed his belly, licked his lips. “Appetite’s growin’ by the minute.”

Wendell considered telling him to get his own damn chili since the bracelet no longer hindered his freedom. But then the game would be “Let’s Make a Death Wish!” Still, he wouldn’t play until he threw out a requirement of his own, a reasonable one.

“All right, I’m going. But first, I need to make sure Drake’s okay.”

“Man, you ain’t in no position to make demands!”

“I don’t get to see my brother, I don’t play.” Despite the childish sentiment of his words, Wendell folded his arms again, valiantly trying to represent determination.

"Boy surprises me more and more!" Ben ruffled his hair. "Fine, let's go see your bro. Though, tell you the truth, Wendy, guy's kinda an asshole. Hardly worth all the effort."

To an extent, Wendell agreed, but blood's thicker than water and all that stupid, stupid stuff spouted by people who never had loud-mouthed, trouble-raising brothers.

Ben dropped a hand on Wendell's back, gave him a little nudge down the hallway. For such a bad-ass, Big Ben seemed awfully touchy-feely.

As if reading Wendell's mind, Ben suddenly retracted his hand and said, "You're all sweaty. I swear, hygiene of a pig or somethin'."

Wendell walked down the wide hallway, Jiggy on his left, Bodacious on his right. Just like in prison death-row movies: *Dead man walking!*

At the end of the hallway, behind a closed door, laughter rose, a man and woman's. When Wendell recognized the man's guffaws as his brother's, he reconsidered his desperate chili run.

Bodacious opened the door and stepped over Napoleon's plastic-wrapped, cumbersome body. Tied to a chair, Drake didn't even notice Wendell, his attention focused on Ben's bimbo. She sat on a chaise opposite him, her ankles crossed, feet wiggling, tapping away on her phone. Giggling as if embroiled in a wondrous flirtation. And Wendell had no doubt that's exactly what had been going on.

Wendell exploded. "Oh, my *God*, Drake! I'm out there fighting for our lives and you're in here hitting up the lady? I should just leave your sorry ass right—"

"Whoa, whoa, slow down, Wendy!" Drake's smile faded. He raised his puffed up eyes to meet Wendell's. Or so Wendell thought; hard to tell through those slits. "I'm not lookin' for a date. Just passin' time, that's all." His gaze wandered the length of Wendell's body. "Why're you naked? What the hell, brah? Wait…did they do something to you? I'll kill 'em!" Flirtatious Drake slipped away. In his place sat the obnoxious, arrogant warrior Wendell needed for their dire situation.

Bodacious stepped forward, slapped Drake. "Best be shuttin' your mouth, bad ass. And you touch Ben's woman, all you all are dead."

The woman fluttered linen-in-the-wind eyelashes. Smiled at Drake, then returned her attention to the phone. Completely unflappable (except for her constantly batting, false eyelashes).

Quickly, Wendell intervened. "I'm sure Drake has no interest in Big Ben's woman. Um, lovely as she is."

"Best not, you know what's right," said Bodacious.

"Drake, they didn't do anything to me," said Wendell. "But, listen…I have to get something for Big Ben. I do this, they'll let us go. And for God's sake, leave the girl alone!"

Wendell turned to his guards, strapped on his serious face—nearly impossible to do in your underwear—and said, "Trust me, Drake's not hitting on this fine, young woman. My brother's just kinda…dumb sometimes. He gets bored easily."

Bodacious and Little Ben grinned, nodded in agreement. The reaction Wendell'd hoped for. He dared to hope things would stay status quo in his absence.

"Dumb? *Me? I'm* not dumb," said Drake, his

testosterone leaking away. “Wendy, don’t do anything for them. Especially if it’s dangerous! Don’t do it if—”

“Yo, man, thought I tole you to shut your hole!” Bodacious jacked his fist up.

Unbelievably, the girl, who’d taken to nibbling the tip of her thumb, injected Drake with a shot of bedroom eyes. Even more amazing, Drake attempted a pathetic wink, ending in an obvious, and well-earned, wince of pain.

Again, Wendell weighed the scales of his brother’s merits, found it plummeting toward the con side. But justice, like love, is blind. Or so say the ubiquitous “they,” who really should just shut up because they don’t know a damn thing.

“I’ll be back, Drake. I’ll get us out of this, I swear I will. Just don’t do anything stupid.” With those words, Wendell left the room before his brother could protest the stupid claim.

Big Ben met Wendell at the door, his clock held out so he could see it. “Tick-tock, tick-tock, you hear time wastin’, Wendy? Two hours now. All the time you got. You have my chili back here by eleven-thirty-two. Or I be makin’ good on my promise.” He hung his head, gripped Wendell’s arm. Stuck his mouth close to Wendell’s ear and whispered, “Good thing I like you, Wendy. Hell, I even liked Napoleon. He was my boy. But your bro? I don’t like him at all. You should see what I do to folks I *don’t* like.”

“I can only imagine.”

“Got that right. Remember, Wendy…No clothes, no money, no help, no calls, no rides, nothin’. We’ll be watchin’.” As Bookes had done earlier, Ben gave Wendell the universally threatening sign of pointed fingers. "Now, go!"

With that, Ben shoved Wendell out the door. Behind him, the door clanged shut, the sound of a tomb closing. But instead of being enclosed within, Wendell never felt more exposed in his life.

Chapter Four

9:35 P.M.

From where Wendell stood—nearly naked on Big Ben's apartment building stoop—his options appeared glum. Go to the police? *No*. Maybe he'd escape with his life, but that left his brother deader than grunge music. Besides, the cops would no doubt arrest Wendell for indecent exposure, hardly a bonus on his resume. Which opened a huge, honking can of worms: How could he get across town in just his underwear and shoes? Doubtful that *Marion's Eats & Drinks* would welcome him with open arms. He envisioned Marion herself (himself?), shaking her head, grimly pointing toward a sign on the wall: *No pants, no service*.

No way around it—he needed clothes, absolutely his first priority. Sure, Big Ben had said clothes were against the rules. But Ben's thugs couldn't watch him every moment. And if he stayed one step ahead of them, dodged them like bullets (and, God, how he hoped that wouldn't turn literal), run like a ghost in the wind, they'd never know.

But how does a naked guy get clothes? Without keys, he couldn't get into his apartment. He didn't know any of his neighbors well enough to bang on their door and ask to borrow clothes. Besides, Ben's fun-loving bunch would be watching.

No doubt about it, he needed help, outside help: Alicia, the only person he could think of, the only person he knew downtown. Of course, after the way things had ended with her, she might be carrying a grudge. A chance he'd have to take.

Pretty much a straight shot, the jog from the Bottoms district to 12th and Brooklyn ordinarily would've been an easy one. But his detour into the Power and Light District—the most popular and crowded downtown partying spot around—would add time and risk. Absolutely unavoidable, though, since that's where Alicia lived.

He rolled the ankle bracelet off his arm, gripped it and stared into the blinking red eye. Maybe if he let the parole cop catch him, he could talk to him, team up with him, save his brother and put Ben and his merry men away. Yeah, right, only in the movies. Bookes wouldn't believe him—probably haul his naked ass in.

Wendell couldn't win. Despair pressed down on him with the unyielding, inevitable dark force of a film noir denouement.

Yet he had to win, had to cross the finish line of the toughest marathon of his life.

With bracelet in hand, Wendell trotted down the steps. Took one last look up and down the street. It appeared vacant, everyone safely—*normally*—tucked into bed, thanks to Ben's tyrannical reign.

As he'd done so many times before, he set out at a deliberately paced, warm-up jog. A cool breeze slapped his back, rushed down his legs, reinforcing his vulnerable state of undress and mind. Across the street, he bounded up onto the sidewalk. The buildings provided plenty of nooks and alleys to burrow into should someone come along.

At 9:40, the West Bottoms had just started to swing, the hipsters out roaming in beanies and bearded packs. Wendell knew the hot-spots to avoid: the coffee houses, bistros, bars, and the winery. Lofts and antique shops closed at night, comprised the majority of the revamped Bottoms, a much safer route of passage for the sartorial challenged. Cloaked within the buildings' shadows, he jogged down the sidewalk. Every time a ribald partying voice from down the street blurted out, he ducked into a doorway, attempting to vanish beneath an awning. Run, hide, repeat…

"*Warning! You have entered a restricted zone! Do you have permission to—*"

"Jesus!" Wendell hopped, skidded to a stop, sure that a SWAT squadron had rifles targeted at him. He saw no one. The bronchial, mechanical squawk continued. The bracelet in Wendell's hand vibrated.

"*Warning! You have entered a…*"

"Great." Wendell shook the device. Smothered it against his belly, and tried to muffle the robotic warning. Unabated, the voice droned on against Wendell's gut, stirring up his already shaken innards. He whacked it against the brick-front of a large revamped warehouse.

Above him, a light flicked on in a second-floor window. A sash drew up, followed by the window.

A bespectacled, soul-patched face popped out. His nose wrinkled, his lips pouted as if smelling something rank. "Dude! You gonna shut that thing up or what?"

"Ahh…would if I knew how. You know anything about ankle monitors?" Any other time, it would've seemed like an absurd question, one Wendell thought he'd never ask. But he saw a brethren soul above him, one who would help him in his time of—

"Man, I'm *not* gettin' involved."

The window slammed shut. The light winked out, a snarky last laugh.

And the voice droned on.

Desperate, Wendell looked about, searching for anything to shut the damn gizmo up. Across the street, an alley with a communal dumpster gave him hope. He darted across the road, and shot down the alley. Glass crunched beneath his sneakers. Dangerous hypodermic needles, no doubt. But his shoes were solid, the ones he usually ran in. Tempted to pet his shoes, invite a healthy dose of good karma, he let it ride. No time for nonsense. He flew down the dark alley, the constant voice babbling in a garrulous manner.

The tall buildings tempered the moonlight. But the unmistakable smell of rotting trash—the sickly sweet odor of dead fruit—led him to the dumpster as sure as a guiding ray of hope. He flung back the lid. Loud as a car's backfiring exhaust, it cracked against the building's wall. Involuntarily, Wendell's teeth snapped shut, nearly as explosive to his ears. Something scurried across his shoe. He yipped, swung his foot up and kicked, an awkward hokey-pokey, until certain the varmint had left. Holding his breath, he leaned over the dumpster. A thin knife of blue moonlight slashed over the contents. No clothing, nothing of use that he could see, at least near the top and he really didn't want to go dumpster digging. Then he saw the bubble-wrap. Not the best solution, but surely it'd help stifle the damned robot. Carefully, he plucked it from the top, shook off something wet and thick that he tried not to give too much thought, and wound it around the bracelet. The voice quieted, but still very audible. Tempted to stomp it to pieces, Big Ben be damned, Wendell raised it above his head, prepared to cry out to the unfair Fates. From behind the dumpster, a cat sprung out, limbs outstretched like a flying squirrel.

"Whoa!" Wendell tottered back, fighting gravity's embrace. The opposite wall caught him, scraping skin from his back. More graceful than Wendell, the cat planted a smooth landing. Its tail whipped back and forth. Wendell backed away slowly, a placating hand out. Apparently assured of Wendell's non-threatening vibe, the cat launched into the dumpster with effortless ease.

"Fine. Your turf, cat," he muttered.

Wendell stared up at the moon, failing to remember what he'd learned in cub scouts about telling time by its position. He ran out of the alley, down to Wyoming street.

Behind him, the distant laughter of partiers rose, likewise raising Wendell's envy. More than anything, he wished he were part of the nightlife scene instead of on this insane nude marathon.

At the corner of Wyoming, he cut behind the Bottoms' only gas station and convenience store, then stopped at the foot of the Twelfth Street Viaduct: huge, daunting, and absolutely impervious in its raised cement glory. The only true way to leave or enter the Bottoms. Always well-trafficked and busy as a freeway, the viaduct posed a huge problem. Sure, the sidewalk provided a nice path for joggers, just not one taken in underwear.

A car wheeled off of Wyoming. Its headlights

slashed over Wendell. The horn blatted. Female laughter mounted into shrieks. Struck like a deer in the headlights, Wendell cupped his hands over his crotch and turned, the way he used to do during high school's torturous dodge ball punishments. Then he dove for the shadows beneath the viaduct's bridge-like structure. He pasted his back against a cement pillar and waited for the lookie-loos to move on. Overhead, cars whooshed by, carrying normal people to normal nighttime situations. A whole lotta cars.

No other option—he had to run beneath the viaduct. Hardly an insurmountable problem. But the hellish hill leading up to downtown Kansas City could be thorny. Literally. Wendell thought about the untamed wilderness, the possible poison ivy and oak lurking on the hill. He rubbed his arms, dreaded the possible outcome to his skin. Usually all he had to do was look at ivy and he'd swell up like the Elephant Man.

Just do it! Quit freaking out and procrastinating and get going! Drake's counting on me. Same brother that got me into this damn mess.

At night, the industrial section of the Bottoms resembled a ghost town. A little creepy, but the isolation suited Wendell just fine. He sprinted down the narrow service street running parallel to the viaduct. Moonlight tinted Wendell's pale skin an icy blue. Goosebumps raced across his arms as if competing in the marathon. Above him, the viaduct rose and rose while the street led him down. His footsteps snapped on the pavement, bouncing off the colossal cement understructure, a chorus line of tap-dancers. Across Mulberry Street, he passed abandoned warehouses, hurtled past the "Edge of Hell," an October-only, spook house event. At Santa Fe Street, the road west ended at a set of railroad tracks. He pulled up short in the gravel. Small pebbles flew up where he dug his toes in.

Somewhere behind him, something clicked: steady, insistent.

Tep, tap, tep, tap…

He held the bracelet to his chest, hoping to once and for all smother the annoying voice. And listened.

Teppity, tap, teppity, tap…

Getting louder. Longer strides, faster pace. Running.

"Ar-yar-yar-yarrr!"

"Christ!"

Big dog. Big, damn angry dog. The dog loped toward him, tongue out. Hair mohawked on its back. Green rings glowed in its eyes, possibly cataracts. But the pissed off dog didn't need to see to eat Wendell.

No time for train-spotting, Wendell high-stepped across the railroad tracks, then scrambled down a slight embankment. Through a knee-high field of weeds, he kicked up his speed. His arms pumped like oil derricks, his legs chopped the weeds like a tractor.

"Nice doggie…good boy…it's all right!" But neither he nor the dog believed it.

The dog's paws slid into the gravel. Its incessant barking grew ferocious, drowning out the cicada call of night.

About one hundred feet ahead, a seemingly unending fence stretched beneath the viaduct. Wendell never knew if the government erected it to keep people in or out of the Bottoms, but now he welcomed it as his escape route, one to separate the men from the dogs.

Uneven, pocked ground impeded Wendell's dash. The jarring course delivered splinters of pain into his knees. At his back, he heard the dog narrowing the gap, flying over the terrain, nothing bothering his knees.

Fifty feet! Faster! Go!

His fists thrust up near his face. His legs stretched, striving for longer strides. Calf muscles yearned for relief as he challenged them. He practically felt—feverishly imagined—the dog's heated savagery on his legs. Closer, closer.

Ten feet! Do it!

A blissful burst of adrenaline primed him for the leap. The unseen dip in the ground didn't. He leapt, bent his legs, expected to land on level turf, then hop up onto the fence. He dropped farther than expected. In a panic, he bobbled. His feet came apart. The impact nearly toppled him over, but he stuck an immediate rebound. All of his weight forced into his lower legs, he jumped up, arms outstretched. The fence rushed toward him.

Clank!

His face smushed against the fence. Fingers interlaced within the chain links. Feet scrabbled to purchase a solid hold. Sprawled across the fence, limbs stretched to the limit, he felt like a bug caught in a web. With the miscalculated second hop, he'd only managed to leap four feet up.

Not high enough. On its hind legs, the dog scrabbled at the fence. The fence clanked and swayed on unsteady posts. Hot breath brushed Wendell's butt. The dog's cold nose tapped his ankle, teeth sure to follow. Terrified to drop his legs, Wendell used only his arms to move up. Arm muscles strained—not the part of the body he'd spent much of his life training. His shoulders rose above his hands, trembling and uncertain. One chance. For a split second, he'd have to let go. Free fall. Trust his arms to jerk up faster than his body could fall into Fido's awaiting jaws. Gravity's bitch.

The dog jumped higher, gaining, settling any niggling doubt Wendell had. He let go. Thrust his arms up. Grabbed the fence and pulled himself to it. Using the momentum, he continued climbing and didn't stop. Clumsily, his right foot groped for a higher toehold before nailing it. At the top, he threw one leg over, then the other, grateful the city hadn't strung barbed wire across the top. In no time, he clambered down the other side. Through the safety net of the fence, he stared down at his nemesis. Now, the dog didn't look so big or scary.

Empowered, Wendell belted out a laugh. "Dog, you suck! Not fast enough for Wendell, are ya?" He drew closer, taunted the dog and shook the fence. "You'll have to be pretty damn fast to put the bite on—"

The dog jumped up, and turned its muzzle sideways. A tooth nicked Wendell's fingertip. Startled, Wendell backed off. "Sorry, sorry… Um, I gotta go."

Once he reached the base of the colossal hill, the thrill of his brief victory evaporated. Covered with bushes, trees, foliage of an indeterminate nature, and no discernible foot trail, the hill appeared as formidable as a mountain. With trash strewn throughout, plastic bags stuck to limbs, flying high like flags. At least mankind had conquered the hill. More than likely, though, people probably just flung their crap from cars as they zipped by on I-35 above. Either way, with a height of 70 feet or so and a slope that would give seasoned mountain climbers pause, Wendell planted a foot, strangled a bush at the base, and started climbing.

He hoped for the best. And by that, he meant a lack of snakes or other critters that could seriously cause harm, and most of all, poison ivy.

****

In a typically lousy mood, Dayton Bookes maneuvered his temperamental Ford Taurus into the Cuckoo Bird Burgers drive-thru line. It's not like he'd been lil' Mary Sunshine before visiting Benjamin Landers—aka "Big Ben"—but every time he thought about Landers running around free, he wanted to put his fist through a window.

Still, he was about to go triple down on a Cuckoo burger, thoughts of it already clogging arteries. No need to let Landers ruin his heart attack on a plate. A nice night, he rolled down the window, inhaled deeply of that loving-like-a-good-dog smell: grease, meat and sizzling onions.

His phone buzzed, a particularly annoying honk, one he downloaded to suit the situation. Chaos about to be unleashed going by the name of Big Ben.

Upon reading the text alert, Dayton grimaced, and kissed his triple burger goodbye. For a while at least. Cuckoo Bird stayed open until midnight. Surely he'd catch up to his guy before then.

Now blocked in, a car practically married to his bumper, Dayton waved his hand at the driver behind him. The guy played dumb, stayed put, and tossed his hands up like Dayton was the idiot.

Dayton laid on the horn, frantically gesturing now.

Screaming out the window for the guy to move. Finally, the guy backed up. Hardly far enough. If Dayton had the time, he would've loved to instill the fear of the badge into the guy, teach him some drive-thru etiquette. But time was wasting, his prey on the loose. Always on call when you're on the job.

After three painstaking reverse, forward, crank the wheel, then repeat efforts, Dayton cleared the bumper ahead of him and swung out of line. He pulled up next to his newfound pal, rolled down the window, and said, "I'm a cop, jackass. Enjoy your burger." Then zipped into a parking spot.

The phone buzzed again, particularly impatient tonight.

"All right then, Benji, let's just see what your dumb ass is up to." Sent by the security company riding shotgun over Landers' ankle monitor, the text alert noted that Benjamin Landers had taken a runner. Typically, no follow-up info. As usual, the true work fell on Dayton's large shoulders.

Frankly, Dayton had a hard time understanding Landers' runaway status. Sure, Big Ben was stupid, not nearly as smart as he liked people to believe, but to split right after Dayton'd paid a personal home visit? Dumber than a flock of geese in a blizzard as Dayton's mother used to say. Or maybe just spoiled by the cushy legal system, buying into his invulnerable hype.

The GPS attuned to Landers' anklet sparked alive after rolling through its ancient warm-up rituals. The blip that represented Benjamin Landers—and, really, that's all the punk was, nothing more than a little blip and a huge pain-in-the-ass to Dayton—blinked off and on like a beacon in the night. On the move.

With a weary sigh, Dayton clunked his car in reverse and left the parking lot with one last forlorn look at the burger place that wasn't to be.

****

9:53 P.M.

No wonder they call it the Bottoms. That was a hellava climb.

Even though Wendell set some sort of speed record climbing through the mess of the hill, he'd lost valuable time. Not to mention a little blood. Scratched up worse than if he'd tussled with the alley cat, his body resembled a road-map of red streets and bruised highways. He'd regretted every painful moment. No matter if he had to go running back down the viaduct in his undies, four minutes of embarrassment seemed like nothing compared to the hell he'd just endured.

Panting, sweating, his tighty-whities adhering uncomfortably to his buttocks, he stood at the peak of the hill, looking down at the endless, flowing traffic of I-35 highway.

Crap. Doesn't anyone ever sleep in this town?

A little bit to the South, I-35 rose a bit. The cement wall bracing the hill conversely lowered into a shorter, safer spot that would drop Wendell onto a narrow strip of grass. Not very wide. He'd have to stick the landing or become road kill. The small matter of crossing four lanes filled with speeding, death-dealing cars and trucks further complicated things.

Massive sign post lattices stretched over the lanes, a ladder conveniently on his side. He supposed he could climb it, straddle his way across, then scurry down the other side. Obviously, graffiti artists did it all the time. Ridiculous, though. Besides the obvious danger, it'd be flat-out embarrassing, on display for the world to see. Not to mention time-consuming.

He had to quit thinking about it. Just get across the damn highway. Fast, the only possible way.

Hunkered over for no real reason than he thought it might make him less visible, he followed the wall to its lowest point.

For what seemed like an endless time suck, he waited for traffic to dwindle. It ebbed and flowed, automobiles flocking together like migrating birds. Except the north and south-bound lanes never synchronized their acts. Ever. Best he could hope for was safe passage across the two north-bound lanes. Then getting stuck on the too-small-for-comfort center median for what could end up a second or hellishly long minutes.

Man, I really don't want to do this.

He couldn't spot any headlights swimming down the north-bound lanes, not for a distance. The break he'd been waiting for. On his stomach, he gripped the wall's edge and swung out. He lowered down the wall's rough-hewn rock side. His fingers released and he fell. To land on his feet, he bent his knees, arms out for balance. His knees butt into the wall, threw him off plan. An unintentional somersault tossed him through the grass and into the highway. His head thudded hard, his upper body laying on the pavement.

"*Dammit!*"

The roar of cars approached, from the north or south he couldn't tell. He didn't wait to find out. He rolled over, jumped to his feet, one foot on the grass strip, the other on the highway. Dizzy. A car sped toward him, headlights glowing. Wendell jagged across the two lanes, his feet barely hitting the pavement. A rush of wind, heat from the car, whipped at his back and lifted his hair. The driver's horn blared, loud on the open lanes, until the sound died once the car vanished around the highway's curve.

Terribly uncomfortable, Wendell straddled the median barrier, his tenuous, temporary safety island. The cement felt rough against his thighs. On display for all to see, he gripped the barrier hard as if riding a bull machine in a bar. Horns blurted, blatted, razzed him. Facing the south-bound traffic, humiliation trumped his fear. White blobs of faces zipped by, some laughing, some dumbstruck at his ludicrous situation. He waited, valiantly (and somewhat ridiculously) trying to keep his chin up.

Traffic died. He swung his other leg over, wasting no time crossing the two lanes. Up another small hill and he finally reconnected with the end of the viaduct, a path he could've easily tore up in minutes.

Although he'd put the physically most demanding leg of his marathon behind him, the most dangerous part of the journey awaited him. This time of night, even on a week night, Kansas City would be alive, full of party-goers or predators, depending on the area. He had to run the gauntlet, run fast, never stop running, just to stay in front of everyone.

At the top of 12th Street, he took advantage of a poorly lit and nearly deserted parking lot and hid in the shadows. With his back against a wall, he watched the traffic move up and down 12th through the Quality Hill district. Somehow, he had to move over to 14th and Baltimore for his detour, the hub of hipsters, a booming area. He'd need to be sly, stick to the darkness like a bat, zoom in and out of peoples' radar.

Anything for pants.

Once he saw a lull in traffic, he dashed through the parking lot, hooked a sharp right onto a street with no name. One he'd never seen, let alone been on before. A dark street, the kind parents always warned against.

While the street's darkness provided a welcome cloak of invisibility, it likewise could hide the more unsavory elements of urban nightlife. Gentrification had started eating up this unsung part of downtown, frameworks of buildings jutting up like skeletons clawing out of their graves. The renewal hadn't made it to the sidewalks yet, old and jagged in spots. Streetlamps were non-existent, civilization not yet staked out fully. Like an explorer in uncharted territories, Wendell crept down the sidewalk slowly, his gaze moving left, then right, and back again. His footfalls, even though rubber-soled, practically screamed, "Intruder! Naked intruder!" A chill rode his bare back, streamed a warning to his brain. He left the exposed sidewalk and moved closer to the construction site—lots covered in dirt, gravel, and discarded building scraps. Although on uneven turf, he picked up the speed, wanting to get the hell out of there.

"Hey! *Hey*!"

The voice nearly punctured Wendell's heart. He slowed, and stopped. Couldn't see anyone attached to the voice.

"What the hell you *doin*'? Out here all naked and everything?"

Wendell turned around, peered into the darkness. Inside one of the roofless structures, something shifted, clunked. A dark shadow separated from the permanent shadows and shambled toward him.

The voice didn't sound menacing, not really. Merely curious. Maybe Wendell could put the man's curiosity to his benefit.

On the other hand, Wendell had experienced a remarkably crappy run of misjudging people, always giving them the benefit of a doubt. Didn't turn out so well for him in high school. He stepped back onto the sidewalk, under the moonlight, so he could see the man coming.

"So…what're ya doin'?" Like he had a golf ball in his mouth, the man spoke lazily, his words sliding together. Didn't stop him from repeating his question, though. *Seriously* curious. "Said 'what're ya doin'?"

Wendell considered several responses, none of them good. "I'm, um, running." Immediately, he wished he could retract his answer. He shifted gears. "I've, ah, fallen on hard times, I'm afraid. Could you possibly help—"

The man stepped in front of Wendell, pretty much ignoring the concept of personal space. A strangely beef-on-the-grill odor rolled off him. He wielded a large flat of cardboard like a spear. Most of the pockets on his army jacket were torn away. His sporadic beard resembled an animated briar patch. Wrinkles criss-crossed his face in sporadic configurations and odd places that didn't make sense. Glassy eyes, yet stridently attuned on Wendell.

"You makin' fun of me, boy?" A finger poked through the end of his glove and scratched his cheek.

"Of course not, sir. I'm just… Look, I'm in a jam, kinda an emergency situation. If you have any spare articles of clothing, anything at all you could loan me,

I'd greatly appreciate it."

The homeless man staggered back as if someone'd popped him in the jaw. He swept off his knit cap, fanned himself. Dropped his cardboard with a slap to the cement.

"You gotta be kiddin' me," he bellowed to the sky as if God had perpetrated a joke. But Wendell knew, absolutely so, that he was about to be the punch line. "You come down here, ask *me* for clothes? *Me*? I'll be damned!" He laughed, chesty as an awful cold.

"Okay, yeah, I can see where you might take offense. My bad. So, um, I'll just go now." Wendell hitched a thumb behind him, hoped to ride along with it out of there.

The man stopped laughing, killed it with a bullet of silence. Anger wrinkled his face to even more extremes. "You think this is funny or somethin'? You and your high-falutin' words and holier than thou attitude comin' onto my turf, makin' fun of me?" He popped a surprisingly strong finger into Wendell's chest.

Wendell retreated a couple steps back, peace-waving hands up. "No, no, no! Seriously, I meant no disrespect! Honestly! I feel for the plight of the homeless! Really! I—"

"Do ya now? Funny damn way of showin' it! You think it's funny to beg from me? That it, smart boy? What, you on some sorta frat initiation? That all we mean to you?"

"Absolutely not! See, my brother—"

Tumph. The man shoved Wendell's shoulder.

"Don't wanna hear 'bout your college brothers, none of that shit!" His voice rose, no longer garbled and mushy, but precise with a razor's edge. "It surprise you

I graduated college, top of my class? Huh?"

Kinda. "Of course not. I really apologize, sir. It's all just a huge misunderstanding. I'll leave—"

Fumph. Another shove, much stronger. Wendell wobbled back, arms pin-wheeling.

"You say you feel for the homeless? Huh, sonny boy? Other than making funna us? You gonna take me to dinner or somethin'?"

"As you can see, I'm hardly dressed to take anyone to dinner right now." Wendell tried on a smile. Colossally bad move. The man pressed in, his hands tightening into fists. "But I'll be glad to come back and—"

"Make funna me again? No chance, boyo!" One more shove, one for the road. Wendell tottered off the sidewalk, spun, and kept going.

Over his shoulder, Wendell called back, "I really will make it up to you, sir! I'll bring a bag of burgers here tomorrow!" In the heat of the moment, in the fire roasting on the pit of menace, Wendell meant it, too.

"Goddamn sumbitch!" the man screamed. "Marge! Major Dent! Ty! *Everyone*! Goddamn, smartass college kid's makin' funna us."

As Wendell took to the center of the street, a quiet buzz built around him. Stereophonic danger. Bodies crawled out of hidden holes, shoved aside sheetrock, and unfolded from shadows. From out of the guts of future abodes for the privileged rose an army of the homeless.

"What's goin' on, Ed?" a woman hollered out.

"That damn naked kid, that's what!" Wendell's homeless nemesis, Ed, addressed his rising masses. "Come down here, beggin' for clothes, like we're some kinda joke to him. Goddamn fraternity prank, that's all we are to him! Let's teach him a lesson!"

"Yeah!"

The buzz swarmed into a furor of screams, grunts and threats. Behind Wendell, a guy loped into the street, a shuffling clop to his gait. Amidst rallying cries, Ed's voice soared louder than the rest, serious chippage on his shoulder. More soldiers joined the chase. If it hadn't been for their menacing intent, it sounded like any marathon: the tread percussion of a band of runners.

Of course, Wendell could outrun a gaggle of homeless. Surely he could. *Right*?

Even though it threw off his stride, he turned half-way around to look, just had to. A couple guys gaining on him. *Easily*. The frontrunners carried bits of construction they'd liberated from their makeshift homes, pipes, two by fours. Ed still with his cardboard. An angry mob, surprisingly swift on their feet.

How come I never knew the homeless worked out?

Up ahead, 12th street. Only way out. Give him public mortification over death. Wendell turned right. He didn't slow, overshot into a wide arc, costing precious seconds. But he'd make it up in a straight sprint. He had to.

Oh my God, oh my God, oh my…

His knees picked up higher, maxing out the limits of his leg muscles. His feet landed violently, yet powerful enough to propel him farther, faster. Hands open, cutting down on wind resistance. Every little bit helped.

"There the lil' bastard goes!"

"Down 12th Street! Get him!"

The straightaway on 12th allowed Wendell to put

some distance between them, but not nearly enough. He envisioned a news report sensationalizing his being bludgeoned to death by a bunch of homeless people. In his underwear. Tough to explain to his parents.

Oh my God, I'm gonna die! Please don't let me die! I don't wanna die! I'll do anything, work in soup kitchens, adopt kittens, hang out with Grandma…

Renovated apartment buildings and lofts comprised the next block of 12th. Inexplicably, the streets were void of human traffic, a helluva time for people to become homebodies. He could try one of the doors to the living quarters, maybe ditch his angry mob. But the buildings were all probably locked up tighter than Dad's liquor cabinet. And life-critical seconds would be snuffed out.

Crossing 12th, he risked another look behind him. Ed had fallen to the middle of the pack, still ranting, still inciting riot conditions. A couple of the younger-looking guys pulled ahead, their forms good enough to compete.

A horn blasted. Wendell faced forward, his pace blisteringly fast. A car approached. Brakes squealed. Wendell leaped onto the sidewalk, and kept going. The car fishtailed to a stop.

The driver yelled, "Goddammit, watch where you're goin'! Get a job, ya freak!"

The car provided a miraculous blockade, slowing down the two fastest men. Instead of running around it, Wendell heard the men pound the car, harass the driver, scream at the guy to move. Their city, their rules. Tires squealed as the car sped away.

With a growing lead, Wendell hooked a sharp left onto Pennsylvania. On downhill runs, Wendell had learned to not get cocky, not to pour on the speed. Many inexperienced runners end up flat on their faces, the momentum driving them into asphalt-kill. But rules were made to be broken, just as long as his bones wouldn't be broken, thank you very much. He ran faster, and rocketed into the downhill trajectory. Using it, owning it.

More apartment buildings—made of brick and greed—lined both sides of the street, crammed close to one another like sardines in a can. Not a lot of hiding spots. Better to keep running, keep moving. Don't get trapped.

But the two die-hard homeless guys kept coming. They stampeded onto Pennsylvania behind Wendell, their hard shoes chock-chock-chocking on the sidewalk.

"You're dead, college boy!"

"Show you to make fun of us!"

Oh my God, I'm gonna die! I just know it! I'm too young to die! I can't…

Sideways, his left leg dragging him through, Wendell squeezed between two parked cars. He cut across the street at an angle. More parked cars crowded the opposite street side, nearly bumper to bumper. Rather than slowing to sidle between them, he sped up. Jumped. One foot landed on the hood of a car, the other followed.

First foot up, clear the car, other foot coming in, joining. Planted it!

The car alarm blasted, insistent as a heart attack. Lights went on in the facing building. Wendell froze, out-of-breath, out of ideas.

Across the street, Wendell's pursuers paused to daintily squeeze between the parked cars, the rage driving them on temporary hold. The rest of the mob entered the street, slowed down to a leisurely jog.

One of the forerunners pointed at Wendell. "He's over there! By the car alarm!"

"Nail his ass," called out Ed.

With that, Ed's warriors rallied. Cheers flared. So did fists and ramshackle weapons. Only thing missing were burning torches and pitchforks. Wendell felt a sudden kin-ship to Frankenstein's monster.

Above Wendell, a window ratcheted up on rusty springs. A voice said, "Not my car." The window closed.

Go, Wendell, go!

Goosing himself, Wendell lit off. Upcoming on his right, an alley, practically hidden behind several trash cans. He grabbed the edge of the brick wall, slowed, hopped, and skipped to a forced stop. Two steps back and he dashed into the darkness.

The alley provided little room to maneuver, hardly wide enough for one person to walk down, a slim person at that. The nature of KC's downtown gentrification plan: use up every available inch of space for primo real estate.

About halfway down, an even smaller alley branched off on the right. Without considering the possibility of being trapped like a rat, Wendell darted in. Forty feet in, the path ended at a brick wall with black iron spikes decorating the top. Next to a dented trash can, debris spread across the ground, boards, flattened boxes, a mess. He stopped, considered bowing back out. But the crowd approached, footsteps and shouts growing louder. Where the hell were the cops? Not that he could afford to be caught, but honestly, he paid his damn taxes.

He spotted a doorway inset into the building on the right. One step up and he pasted his back against the metal door. The doorknob nudged his side, the metal freezing on his back and legs.

Swift-footed as ever (*Who are these guys? Disgraced Olympians?*), the two men slapped soles past the alley. Wendell held his breath. He'd be doing it for a while. Seconds later, more of the mob dashed by, clomping stiffly down the sidewalk. Then the tidal wave of the crowd moved past—as in any marathon, the majority located in the middle, running out of gas, but still trudging along.

"Think he went down there?"

"Nah," Ed's voice rang out, "even that asshole wouldn't be that stupid."

Endless shuffling, loud breathing, flung loogies, voices—some pissed, others apparently enjoying the outing—paraded past the alley. A terrifying parade.

Finally, the largest grouping passed. But Wendell knew the procession hadn't finished yet. Now would come the laggards, the fatties, the three-pack-a-day smokers, shuffling half-heartedly to the finish line. Some even given up and walking. He wasn't in the clear, not by a long shot.

Carefully, with baby-steps, Wendell grabbed the doorknob. Sweaty palms—a predicament Wendell suffered a lot to his chagrin—loosened his grip. His hand slipped away, thumped into the metal. Again his bowels surged. He winced, closed his eyes, and hoped the noise had been lost on the crowd. He wiped his palm against his underwear (which also felt pretty sweat-soaked), and tried the knob again. Resistance.

Locked.

"Dammit," he whispered.

"*Hey*! What're you *doin'* in there?"

Wendell's heart nearly exploded, something he thought wouldn't happen for another fifty years. The voice startled him; loud, slurred, and all too easily peggable as one of the homeless army.

At the back of the alley, in front of the wall, the trash can rattled. Something swished, boards moved aside.

"Who's there?"

Wendell stepped out of his cubby-hole. Sure enough, another homeless man crawled to wobbly legs, prepared to defend his brick wall. He appeared dazed, presumably awoken from sleep. Like a toddler, he rubbed a curled fist in his eye.

"*Please* keep your voice down." Wendell tried to dredge up the proper amount of respect and forcefulness, but an impossible task to pull off in a whisper.

Naturally, the man didn't comply. "You don't belong here!"

At Wendell's back, footsteps approached. Stopped. A murmured voice.

Pointlessly, Wendell held a finger to his lips, quietly uttered, "Shh, shh…"

"Hey," yelled Wendell's new roommate, "you out there! You lookin' for this guy?" He stuck out a shaking finger toward Wendell. "Hey! He's here!"

A voice called into the alley. Far away sounding, yet nightmarishly close. "That smart-ass college kid in there, Chester?"

"Sure is!" said Chester.

“Crap,” said Wendell. He peered into the darkness, assessing his odds. Streetlight backlit two figures as they slowly—*warily?*—approached him. He couldn’t discern their size, gender, anything. It didn’t matter; he never was a fighter.

Impossible to scale the brick wall. Not all that tall, really, just about twelve, thirteen feet. But no handholds. And the spikes definitely counted on the downside.

Then he noticed, on the opposite wall, another door inset into the building.

Dear God, let it be open, then I swear, absolutely, I’ll donate tons of money to the homeless, and—

Wendell squeaked a bit as the knob twisted in his hand. Down the alley, the two stragglers threw caution to the wind and advanced faster. Chester just stood there, arms folded, presumably pissed off he’d been awakened.

Wendell slipped through the door, and closed it. Fumbled in the dark for a lock. His finger slipped into an old-fashioned keyhole, the figure-eight kind.

“Gah! Who *uses* these anymore?”

Wendell careened down the dark hallway. Like a pinball, he bumped into the walls, going nowhere and hoping for an escape hatch.

Behind him, the doorknob rattled. Voices mounted in the alleyway, the mob amassing for round two.

At the end of the hallway, a small sliver of welcome light crawled across the floor. Wendell dashed toward it, found another doorknob. He opened it, and went through it just as his pursuers entered the hall behind him. Again, he sought out a lock and found yet another one of those ridiculously outdated keyholes. So much for the 21st century.

A flight of stairs led up, delivering him to the source of light. Two stairs at a time, Wendell flew. And opened another door.

A sudden flood of light dazzled him. A church, big, open and lit with an array of bulbs recessed into the arched ceiling. Smaller interior arches emulated the arch formation of the stained glass windows.

Beautiful! Nothing bad can happen in church! I mean, right?

The item on the altar really caught Wendell's eye.

He raced up the two wide, curved steps. Next to the wooden lectern, behind the priest's chair, stood a typically somber, possibly gold-plated rendition of Jesus hanging on a cross. Draped over the horizontal arms of the cross and behind Jesus hung a long cloth. It'd make a fine toga.

Yet guilt weighed him down. Jesus' tortured eyes glared at him. *Followed* him. Although never much for religion, he certainly believed in Karma, both kinds. Definitely not the time to tempt Karma, particularly when he could use a solid dose of the good stuff.

He wheeled, ready to race down the steps and flee between the rows of pews to naked freedom. Instead, he froze. Stared into the gaping black mouth of a shotgun. A clearly irritated priest stood behind the weapon.

"Um, I come in peace?" said Wendell.

"You here to rob the church again, *boy*? Get your drug money by stealing from the Lord?" *Ka-chak!* "Not on my watch, *crack-head*!"

As Wendell looked into the long barrel of the shotgun, a crazy thought rattled his addled brain: *How come no one ever mentions my naked state?*

Chapter Five

10:06 P.M.

Dayton Bookes knew something was up. Or rather down, going way down, bottom floor down. The Cathedral of Saint Mary hardly seemed like Benjamin Landers' typical hangout. Why in hell would Landers risk going to prison for some good ol' fashioned come to Jesus moments when he could turn on the TV, catch the televangelist of the moment?

He wouldn't. Doubtful redemption topped Landers' things-to-do list.

Yet, the GPS screen didn't lie. Landers' blip winked at Dayton, the physical address right there in eyestrain green on black.

As always in these refurbished neighborhoods, parking spots were sewn up tight. One opening remained, although a no parking sign designated it as off-limits. Dayton couldn't really see a reason why; it didn't block any fire hydrants, driveways, nothing. Just bureaucratic bullshit. Red tape he didn't mind snipping. And if any damn meter maid tried to ticket him for doing his job, he'd have words. Lots and lots of bad words. He hadn't forgotten the burger that got away yet.

Only thing is, some yuppies crammed a Prius and Lexus as close to the sign as possible, leaving very little space for his Taurus. Of course, Dayton'd be the first to admit he absolutely sucked at parallel parking. Sorta a sissy sport created by people with lots of spare time on their hands. Way too time-consuming and stressful.

Hey, fugitive at large and all. Dayton didn't fancy becoming a media scourge should Landers go on a shooting spree.

Dayton maneuvered the car sideways, faced the spot head-on, and pulled onto the curb. The Taurus' back end stuck out in the street and, as if defying him, its tailpipe banged out a pop. Stupid car. All the KCMO PD would give him even though he spent most of his job driving from parolee to parolee.

He banged the glove box with his knuckles (the handle having gone belly up long ago), adding a new dent among all the other battle wounds. Wadded up parking violations, a bag of Gummi Bears (best thing since cigars), and his gun avalanched to the floor. He picked up his Glock .40 caliber automatic, checked it, made sure a bullet filled the chamber. Smiled. At least the department didn't skimp on his gun.

Dayton left the car, and didn't bother to lock it. Neighborhood like this, he kinda hoped it'd get stolen. He hid the gun in his shoulder holster—no need to start an unnecessary panic. But with Landers, just like the scouts say, it pays to be prepared. A real live-wire, that guy. These days, though, the law had to be more careful than the crooks.

With his forefingers locked into his belt loops, he hitched up his slacks, and followed through with the back. Damn things never did want to conform to his body. At a bar, someone once suggested he wear suspenders. Dayton asked the guy how he'd like to wear his fist in his mouth.

The church's flight of steps winded him, certainly not created with big men or little old church ladies in mind. His hand on the rail, he took a moment. Wiped his sleeve across his forehead. Opened the outer door.

He entered the alcove, and yanked open the second door. In the lobby, water bubbled and popped in the Baptismal Font. Over the sound of the percolating water, he heard two voices.

One final set of heavy doors to contend with (*church ladies must have arms of steel*) and he prepared for anything. Just not the horror he witnessed playing out in front of the altar. He froze, jaw hanging, one hand holding the door open, the other hand instinctively wanting to pull the gun yet afraid he might shoot his own eyes out.

The kid—the "Strawberry" from Landers' loft—stood in his underwear, hands up, pleading by the looks of things. A ruddy faced priest held him at gunpoint, his shotgun nearly as big as he was.

The hell? Figure it out later.

Afraid to take his eyes off the bizarre tableau for even a second—and that's all it'd take for the kid to turn into strawberry jam—Dayton fumbled and searched for his gun. He missed the first two attempts, his hand sliding down inside a tear in his jacket's liner. Third time he nailed it.

"Both y'all freeze now." Not too loud, quietly commanding, trying to keep beautiful sanity alive.

The priest turned his head but the gun remained locked on Strawberry's chin. Hands in the air, praising Jesus, Strawberry slowly stepped back. He held something wrapped in plastic in one of his fists.

Gun out, arms locked, Dayton supported one hand beneath the other. Practically a hostage situation, he cautiously made his way down the aisle. "Father, what say we put the shotgun down?"

"You here to rob the church, too?" The priest's nostrils flared. A tuft of gray hair on his head stood up, waggled like seaweed.

"I'm Police Officer Dayton Bookes. Once everyone gets nice and cozy without all the guns, I'd be tickled to flash my badge. How 'bout lowerin' the gun now, Father? Doubt Jesus would approve." He wagged eyebrows toward the disapproving Jesus statue.

"This lowlife scum tried to rob the church *blind*," said the priest. "For drug money!"

"That's *not* true," protested Strawberry. "See, I got—"

Suddenly, other voices rose, loud as a revival meeting, though Dayton saw no one. For a second, he wondered if the Rapture were upon them. Nothing else made sense.

A side door cracked open. A pageant of homeless people stormed out, raced toward the altar. Angry with arms up, they brandished sticks, boards, broken bottles. Strawberry darted up onto the altar, ducked behind the priest's chair.

Startled, the priest stumbled back and tripped on the first altar step. As he went down, his gun went up.

Bla-blam!

Heavenly plaster crashed down upon the homeless mob.

Jumpin' Jesus Christ—sorry 'bout that, Jesus—what's going on now?

Gun tightly fisted in hand, Dayton hustled toward

the crowd. Cleared his throat and unleashed his formidable baritone. "*Everyone*, calm down *now*! I'm *police*! Got a gun and badge and everything! Everyone lower your weapons. Slowly… That's right. Good. Liked how you did that, nice moves. Uh-huh…"

For the most part, the crowd complied. They chunked the weapons into a central pile, some flat-out heaving them from a distance. A lot of them meandered around, dumbfounded and docile, as if awakening after a bout of sleepwalking.

Guy in the middle, though, still ranted on, waving around a short two-by-four. "*Dammit*—sorry, Father—that kid in his underwear tried to *roll* me!"

"Put down the big stick and we'll talk about it." While Dayton pointed his gun up, he made sure he'd have a quick drop on the angry guy, the biggest threat. *Maybe*. Damned if Dayton could put it together.

"And he tried to rob the church, too!" The priest stood, patting down the backside of his robe. "We want justice! Old testament! Eye for an eye!"

"Yeah! Pull out his eyes!" hollered the ringleader. "When're you cops gonna do your job, get the *real* criminals? Just cause he's rich and white, don't mean he's a saint!"

And here we go…

"Folks, folks…" Patronizing hands, one loaded with gun. "Race isn't an issue here. You see I'm black, right? Only color I care about's evil. Now, let's start over. Someone wanna tell me what happened?"

"That…that *kid*! He started *everything*," said the guy with the stick. "Arrest his punk-ass!"

"Well, I'll get to him. But let's leave the justice to me. Now…where is the Strawberry?" On tiptoes,

Dayton peered over their heads, up into the altar. Hoping the Strawberry would pop out on command. So much for optimism.

Quiet filled the church, the way all churches should be in Dayton's opinion.

Then, "There!" A woman pointed a gnarled finger toward the back of the church. "He's getting' away again!"

Dayton swung around just in time to see the church's door shut. Hungry and tired, Dayton groaned.

Well, dammit... Lil' bastard's gonna make me chase him.

****

10:09 P.M.

Wendell crashed through the church doors, one arm stuck out like a quarterback cradling a football. He hurdled down the stairs, his feet rolling them off in a dangerous yet speedy manner, and back into the night.

With the commotion caused by the parole cop and the mob, it'd been easy to sneak out through the church. Before he'd left, he glanced at a painting of Mary. Glum, she glared down at him as if saying: *For shame, Wendell*! Add Mary, Jesus, and Bookes to his battlefield of opponents.

Welcome to war-torn downtown, KCMO.

No more messing around. He had to get down to 14th and Baltimore. *Pronto*. Assuming Alicia'd be home, of course. And not still pissed off at him.

At the bottom of the stairs, he turned left on 12th, the passing traffic hardly a concern any longer. Once you've come close to death, underwear embarrassment sort of seemed so-been-there, done-that.

According to the church dome clock, he'd already

lost nearly half of his allotted time. He couldn't afford any more setbacks. Nothing but running, what he excelled at.

He crossed the street—always diagonally, every shortcut helped—and shaved a little time through another parking lot on the corner of 12th and Washington. The abundance of parking lots signified two things: 1) parking lots provided nifty shortcuts for running, naked men; 2) parking lots meant more civilization, more nighttime carousers out and about. The next stretch of his run could be done in minutes, mastered in a mere two straight shots. If unimpeded. Streaking through throngs of night people and patrolling cops carried a few potential setbacks.

He could do it; hell, yeah, he could do it. But it involved risk. Strangely, the longer his nightmare progressed, the less risk seemed to bug him.

Do it.

In another large parking lot, he took to the back wall and rushed through an abbreviated stretching routine. No sense riding the Charlie Horse the rest of the way. He touched his toes a dozen times, maintaining his legs as straight as possible. Against the wall, he pressed his fingertips, extended his butt, stretched one leg behind, then switched. Repeated the move several times as his underwear crawled uncomfortably between his cheeks. Again, worst day ever to blow off laundry. Had he been wearing boxers or even boxer briefs, people could easily mistake them for workout shorts. Maybe, sorta if they were half drunk and blind.

Time to go.

Deep breath, a couple more, and…

Wendell utilized the cover of the parking lot for the entire block. He raced between the rows of cars. Next to him, a car beeped. Involuntarily, he beeped back, an effeminate shriek. Footsteps chocked down the sidewalk toward him, steady, evenly paced, not the army of enraged homeless. As he hauled out of the parking lot, he passed a guard in a booth (who didn't even flinch, immediately returned to his phone), hurdled a low-hanging chain, and reached the intersection at 13th street.

The stoplight stayed stubbornly red, but as the cool kids in high school (not that he'd ever run with them, natch) said, "No cop, no stop." As he raced through the intersection, far down on 13th street, a lone car rumbled, a hungry lion. The headlights flared to bright. Tires squealed leaving a signature of rubber behind as the car rocketed toward Wendell.

He cleared the intersection with a wide stride, parachuted onto the sidewalk. Karma decided to pay him back for the church business: *No Parking* signs lined both sides of the Washington block. No safety buffer of cars between him and the street. Likewise, the sidewalks butt right up to the old buildings and shuttered businesses. Any place he could run, a car could follow. He lit out down the sidewalk, chest heaving, arms and legs jacking.

Behind him, the car overshot its target of Washington. Brakes locked up, another screech of tires while it spun into reverse.

The car roared down Washington, rap music aggressively cranked. Above the music, Wendell distinguished shrill laughter, akin to a witch's cackle. *Little Ben.*

Wendell stopped, hands on knees, breathing hard, head up to face his "cheerleaders."

The tricked-out Chevy Impala jerked up, the tail end bouncing up and down. Behind the steering wheel, Bodacious locked the brakes, his preferred driving method.

Jiggy leaned out the back window, and said something. Wendell couldn't hear him over the music. He put hands over his ears, blatantly showing the thugs his brain was exploding. The music lowered, still loud enough to resonate within Wendell's chest.

Little Ben leaned across Bodacious, said, "What 'chu doin', Wendy? Should be runnin' to save your bro."

"I'm *trying*."

"Don't look like it to me."

For no reason Wendell could fathom, Bodacious hit the Impala's hydraulics, bounced the car again.

"Look, I'm doing the best I can here! I—"

"What you doin' at church anyway?" asked Little Ben. "Lookin' for handouts? Maybe clothes or some shit?"

"What? Course not! I'm playing by the stupid rules!" Wendell dragged up what indignation he could, then softened the blow as he remembered who the opposing players were. "Just avoiding the law any way I can. You know how it is."

Bodacious nodded, took his sunglasses off and showed Wendell his lazy eye. Clearly the reason why the guy wore sunglasses at night. Definitely the worst driver choice, though. On the other hand, if Bodacious got them into a wreck, Wendell wouldn't lose any sleep over the accident.

"Get your ass goin', Wendy," said Little Ben. "Your bro's dead if you don't make curfew."

Wendell sighed. "Maybe if you'd *let* me get going, then—"

"Know what they did back in the olden days to make horses run, Wendy?" While Wendell's gut answered in a silent scream, *You're not gonna like this,* Little Ben said, "Show him, Jiggy."

"Gonna show him, G." Jiggy leaned out the window, his belly perched on the sill, one arm hidden at a contortionist's angle behind him. Somehow he finagled a whip out of the car. Several leather strands at the whip's tail-end dangled beads, clacking against the car door. With an arm-straining thrust, Jiggy lashed the whip tail over the car. A micro-second away from slashing it into Wendell.

Wendell ran. The whip snapped behind him, ice cracking across a winter pond.

"Jesus!" Wendell careened down Washington, hoping to make it to the crowds of 14th Street. The car lurched after him, halted with a squeal of bad brakes. Repeatedly drove that way like a student driver, leisurely—playfully—chasing Wendell.

"Get *him*," Little Ben cried, no longer in the mood to play. The whip snapped again, popped the air.

Ahead lay the intersection of Washington and 14th.

Twenty feet…*snap*!…ten feet…*crack*!

A still night, Wendell swore he felt the wind of the whip at his back. The car crawled behind Wendell, start, stop, start, stop. Jiggy honed his skills, drawing the whip's tail closer.

At the corner, Wendell cut sharp, hopped over a small embankment, and scraped his left arm on the building's brick front. Tore across three empty parking spots and landed on the sidewalk.

Ahead, headlights swarmed like lightning bugs. Nighttime revelers strolled both sides of 14th Street. Terrible for keeping a low profile. Wonderful to avoid the taste of a whip. Wendell doubted the wrecking crew would be so stupid as to chase him down the street with a weapon hanging out the window.

As suspected, the Impala stopped at the intersection. The engine grumbled, disappointed. Breathless, Wendell watched the car pull a slow U-turn. Little Ben's grating voice shrieked, "'Member, Wendy…we got eyes on you! We know where you at!" The red taillights faded down the street, blinked out over a hill.

Wendell leaned against the building, catching his breath. Rattled, trembling. The adrenaline rush he could put to good use.

Ahead lay the most dreaded lap of his impromptu marathon. But unlike in marathons, he intended to take it at a mad sprint, not his usual steady, deliberate pace. Three blocks of Kansas City nightlife: couples strolling arm-in-arm, people riding bikes, dog walkers, some joggers (all fully clothed, of course, and he was gonna *so* smoke them), an army of looky-loo's and phone video archivists, and worse…cops cruising the street.

The first block didn't look so bad: empty cars lined both sides, ample sidewalks next to them. No hiding spots, though, just unsheltered parking lots. On foot, a few people headed away from Wendell toward the hub of the city. Through which Wendell had to run.

He felt time escaping him like air siphoning out of a balloon, inevitable. One last stretch against the wall, left leg back, then the right leg. Ready…

Go!

His feet slapped down the sidewalk, a slight decline propelling him faster. Ahead of him walked a sharply dressed couple. Even though a warm night, the woman wore gloves, her jacket collar up; theatre-goers. To avoid them, Wendell zagged across the street, and hopped a low-slung chain into a parking lot. Fists up and churning butter, he tore across the macadam, jumped the chain on the opposite side. Once he put a reasonable distance between him and the couple, he cut back over to the northern sidewalk, the one with better shadow coverage. Behind him, the man laughed. Not exactly the response Wendell expected, but also not an alarming distress call either. Small favors.

Just ahead lay Broadway in all its street-lit, car zooming, horn-honking glory. At the sight of the vibrant life, Wendell felt his glory shrink a little bit.

Just power through it, the only way!

The stoplight turned traitorously red on him. Without slowing, he zipped through the intersection, relying blindly on the drivers' innate goodness not to run him down. A horn blasted. Someone hurled an insult. Business as usual. He leaped onto the sidewalk, legs crunching down hard before lifting off again.

Clusters of people had now amassed into larger groups. On the left, Bartle Hall, KC's biggest exhibition center, stretched out over a half block. Wendell willed more speed into his legs, sped past the enormous glass front lit up like a ballpark. Businessmen and women dressed in jealousy-inducing suits filed out of the building. Some man yelled, "Hey, *hey!*" which struck Wendell as ludicrous. If he'd stopped, turned around, and asked, "Yes?" how would the guy reply?

He kept running, kicking it like he never had before. Like his life depended on it, and frankly, yeah, it did.

As he swerved around a woman, she screamed.

"Sorry, sorry," Wendell called back, his words trailing like dust already lost to the wind.

He wove between people, some in a hurry to get to their cars, others dawdling and mingling in small groupings. Wendell's uttered apologies didn't alleviate his embarrassment or his terror one bit, but they made him feel slightly less pervy.

Faces swam by him at a rapid clip, blurring, morphing together. The exact way, he imagined, fish in an aquarium felt.

Some clown yelled, "Run, Forrest, run," which evoked hearty laughter. Wendell pasted on a pained grin, nodded, took it in stride (so to speak), and ran. Head up, eyes straight ahead. Cheeks burning red, the other cheeks practically hanging out. He'd been the butt of many jokes before, but never like this, not with his butt as the joke. More laughter pursued him. Sometimes temptation's an enticing mistress. Several times he wanted to stop, yell at these uncaring ass-hats, exclaim proudly how his was a noble mission. "Look, this isn't my choice! I have to get chili!" But they wouldn't understand. Nor would time.

Wendell conjured more speed, calling on a nearly mystical force. He didn't know where it came from, but gladly embraced it when it breathed new vigor into him. He jet across Central, this time with the grace of the green light. Goose honks blatted from cars stopped at the light. His heart pounded out a bass drum solo. A quick scan above car roofs for cop cherries confirmed a temporary all-clear. So far, so good.

His shoes cracked across the sidewalk, echoing off Municipal Hall's large cement structure. Apparently event-free tonight, the building lay dormant, mercifully deader than a monstrous tomb. Yet crowds continued flowing, lemmings milling in the streets, oblivious to the traffic trying to pass through 14th. Apparently, none of them with jobs to go to tomorrow.

Streetlamps lit the block on fire. Anchored into the sidewalk parallel to Municipal Hall, smaller lamps stole the lower darkness away. Wendell plotted a direct course, deviating slightly only to avoid crashing into people. More than ever he felt exposed, his goods practically flapping in the night air. Trapped in the unwanted spotlight. Gasps, a smattering of applause, a couple screamed, mostly hoots followed in his wake. Eyes on the prize and locked dead ahead, definitely not into the eyes of his audience. Occasionally, he turned and broke his rule. In a backward jog, he looked for cops.

As he barreled across Wyandotte Street, the crowd make-up shifted. People gentrification. Men's suits traded down for t-shirts and ironically vintage clothing. Young women wore hats, skinny jeans, or cut-off shorts, the pockets falling below the material. Beanies supplanted expensive hair-styles. Attitudes changed, too. Not necessarily for the better.

"Dude!"

"Forget something man?"

"Whoa! Streaking's so…retro!"

Jam-packed with nightlife, the streets and sidewalks were plugged with hipsters looking to be seen. Wendell reigned in his speed before he bowled a strike of people. He retreated to the parking lots again, off the street and not nearly as crowded.

Screams and guffaws continued to plague him, a wave-like effect. Fingers pointed. Unfunny jokes tossed. He'd had training with this behavior before, wore his rhino skin like insult-deflecting armor.

Focus, dammit! Don't let 'em get to you! Almost there!

With Alicia's apartment building in sight, half a block away, he pushed himself to mad extremes. Jarred by his heavy footfalls, his breath chugged like a train. He opened his mouth, breathed deeply through it, his nose unable to keep up with the needed intake. His teeth clomped together with every planted foot. Arms thrust, hands chopped, shoulders rolled, legs leapt.

To his right a bachelorette party had gathered, clogging up the sidewalk. Squeals and giggles erupted, capable of breaking glass. Most of the girls sported genitalia balloon head gear, hooker pumps, and oddly out of place fur coats. Upon seeing Wendell jag by them, they unleashed a litany of obscenities and mocking catcalls. Their arms went up in the air, first one, then the next as if climbing a rope. Hips swayed.

Then Wendell stopped, his feet absurdly outrunning, skidding past him like in old cartoons. At the intersection of Baltimore and 14th—in front of his safe haven destination—two cops sat on bicycles, stuck in traffic. Probably rent-a-cops, maybe the real deal, didn't matter either way as both would cause Wendell a world of hurt: Do not collect pants, go directly to jail.

Crap!

Wendell ducked behind a parked car. He poked his

head up, saw the cops had wormed through the crowds to the red traffic light. The light changed over, their feet up on the pedals again and headed his way.

Either a giant Hail Mary or a lunk-headed decision, Wendell darted toward the roaming bachelorette party.

“Ladies! Hey ladies,” his voice nearly drowned out by their hubbub, “hey, check me out!”

Without a hint of shame, Wendell bit the bullet and leaped over the parking lot’s chain. He landed next to the girls in a pose, puny biceps flexed, wishing he had more to give. The girls clammed up at the unexpected sighting. Several of them hit him with the familiar high school “sneer face”—lips twisted in a painful-looking, pretzel shape—a look perfected and apparently inherent in all snooty women.

The cops bicycled his way, heads constantly craning for foul play.

Taller than the girls, Wendell hunkered down. “Gather ’round me, girls, come on in, closer. I’m part of the entertainment tonight!” Cautious with his hands, using them like a traffic cop and touching nothing, he corralled the women into a circle around him.

“Kathy, is *this* the guy you hired?” Judging by the mini-skirted wedding dress, the bride-to-be. She held up her arm, finger drooping down at Wendell like the Grim Reaper.

Kathy, her face obscured by trendy glasses, gave Wendell an uncompromising up and down. Lingered a long time over his underwear. “Ew, no! The guy I booked—”

“Ladies, ladies!” Hands waved like a vaudeville comedian trying to avoid tomatoes. “I’m the warm-up. Consider this a freebie!” He smiled. A nervous tic in his eyelid flickered, his poker game giveaway for a blatant lie. “Let’s get this party started!”

Wendell peeked over the women’s heads again. Only feet away now, a large group crossing the street had stalled the cops. But the girls held the cops’ rapt attention. One of them grinned lecherously, so far oblivious to Wendell’s presence.

“I dunno, Kathy…,” said the future bridezilla, “he looks kinda scrawny to me.” Not to be left out, she performed an uncomfortable scan over Wendell. Absentmindedly—Wendell harbored no doubt her usual state of mind—she toyed with her veil, a finger curling the bottom.

“C’mon, girls, let me show you what I got!” Wendell emulated a gorilla stance, arms curled and tight—the way wrestlers did it—trying to force magical biceps he knew he didn’t have. “Hit the music, ladies!”

Another girl produced her phone, found some rap.

Never much of a dancer—his feet only good for straight-up running, never mind the fancy footwork—Wendell latched onto the only dance he knew, and not very well at that. He shimmied his shoulders, searched for a beat. His hips and legs locked, elbows up, his torso bent forward. He dropped his lower arm and let it sway like it’d fallen out of socket. His head tilted to the side, his facial expression frozen in a vacant, nobody-home daze.

“Eww…is that…whaddayacallit? The Robot?” The girls tittered, shrieked. Miraculously they moved in closer. Everyone loves a clown. More power pumping arms raised as they hopped back and forth. As long as they provided coverage, Wendell’d gladly play their jester.

"You ain't seen nothin' yet." Rigidly, Wendell shifted his shoulders, replaced the other arm and let it swing. This time he tilted his face toward the right, head down, but eyes watching the cops as they slowly rode by. Too slowly. Big grins for the women. At long last they passed, off to go fight crime.

Wendell stopped, straightened. "Um, sorry, ladies, show's over."

He shouldered through the circle of women and dashed across Baltimore. Back in predatory mode, the girls flung insults at him.

"Where ya going', ya no-assed weakling?"

"I've seen better moves in a retirement home!"

"Call yourself a *man*?"

The verbal onslaught arrested the surrounding crowd's attention. Well-intentioned—or hoping to get lucky—guys' voices rose in outrage, wondering what the naked guy had done to the damsels in distress. Fingers pointed. Threats aimed. From down the street, a whistle, shrill and high and absolutely the bicycle cops' version of a siren, trilled.

Dashing up the stoop to the Power and Lights Apartment building, Wendell yanked open the outer doors, tossed open the inner doors, and barreled inside. Absolute awe threw the brakes on his sneakers. Disneyland for hipsters, the only way to describe it. From his date with Alicia, he knew she lived in these apartments. While he hadn't actually visited her apartment, he knew of the reputation, and it still didn't prepare him for the ludicrous extravagance. An enormous chandelier shone brilliantly, rays of blinding light shooting from it like lasers. Hanging lamps blazed throughout the vast, art deco inspired lobby, making

Wendell feel like he'd just stepped inside from a sun-struck snowy day. Vaguely aware of other people in the lobby, nothing but bouncing, fuzzy outlines, he wobbled, felt the need to sit down. Overwhelming silence buzzed in his ears like bees.

Then a firm hand landed on his chest, followed by a snidely weedy voice, "Um… *no*," the hand's owner declared.

Chapter Six

10:17 P.M.

Bit by bit, Wendell's vision sorted back into existence. The hand remained on his chest, fingers splayed. A thin, young guy, hair slicked back, painted into a skintight suit with a short jacket and even shorter pants, belonged to the hand. Caterpillar hair riding beneath pursed lips delineated his hipster breeding. The name-tag, pronouncing him "Vincent, your concierge" gave away his intent.

"Just…*no*," repeated Vincent. "You're *not* coming in here, short bus." His hand stayed, strength in those digits. Wendell stepped away, feinted to the side. Vincent countered, a dance partner Wendell had no time for.

"Okay…Vincent. This isn't how it looks. Honestly. I'm not homeless or—"

"And I don't want to hear your sob story." Vincent wailed on his imaginary violin. He gave Wendell a sort of side-long glance, one suited more for public transportation riff-raff. "Soup kitchen's across town. Now leave, short bus. You're disturbing our tenants."

Wendell studied the occupants in the decked out lobby. Hipsters with drinks in hand and amused smirks on their faces, appeared more entertained than disturbed.

"Vincent, again…" Wendell fell back on friendly, patting hands. Not that they'd done him much good tonight. "I'm not homeless. I have a home in the Bottoms. If you'd just buzz Alicia Saunders for me, I'm sure she can—"

"No can do, sport. I don't even *want* to know how you came by Alicia's name—stalking, no doubt your hobby—and I'm *definitely* not bothering Ms. Saunders. Not for the likes of you. Now…" With two fingers, Vincent tweezed out his phone from a snug vest pocket, an aqua polka-dotted affair. "The cops are seconds away. You want a free meal in jail tonight?"

Desperate—absolutely not in his right mind and going farther nuts by the second—Wendell pointed behind Vincent. "Hey! James Franco!"

Bait swallowed, Vincent swiveled, a hand to his gaping mouth. Wendell set off in the opposite direction, dashing across the lobby.

"Stop him! Somebody *stop* him," screamed Vincent.

Behind the lobby desk, another thin goateed man—could've been Vincent's twin—gasped, then snatched up the desk phone. Quietly, he mumbled into the phone. One tenant stepped out of Wendell's path, tilted his beer bottle as if in salute.

At the elevator, Wendell called back, still trying to sound reasonably sane, "Believe me, it's not what it seems."

Wendell punched the up button, kept hammering it. He looked back. Vincent, now allied with his twin, approached. A game of "Green Light, Red Light," they took baby steps then stopped, did it again, slowly closing in on Wendell. The elevator indicator displayed both cars stuck on the seventh floor.

Somehow believing his voice could travel through the elevator hatch all the way up to Alicia's apartment on the seventh floor, Wendell screamed, "Alicia! Alicia Saunders! It's me! Wendell! I know you're up there! I need your help! Alicia! I—"

"Sir! Lower your voice! And stop slapping the button! Lower your hand!" Like Wendell's hand was a dangerous weapon.

"*No!* Alicia!" He beat on the elevator button until his hand numbed. "Alicia! It's Wendell! Please—"

Vincent lassoed a deceptively strong arm around Wendell's neck. The desk clerk swung a leg beneath Wendell's. Wendell plummeted down. On his back, he kicked at the men. As if hating the thought of dirtying his suit pants, Vincent grimaced, then dropped to his knees. He shoved Wendell over onto his stomach, then bound his wrists together. The other guy grabbed Wendell's ankles. Together, they hoisted Wendell up and carried him toward the front doors.

He couldn't give up now. Wendell squirmed, gave the men the fiercest squirming they'd probably ever experienced. A *helluva* squirming.

"Aliciaaa! Alicia Saunderrrs!" Wendell bellowed as the men lugged him away. He sounded like a poor man's Marlon Brando wailing for Stella, but he didn't care. In fact, he didn't care about much of anything. Game over. "Aliciaaa! Aliciaaa! Aliciaaa Saund—"

"*What*?"

All heads turned toward the female voice. An Asian girl stood just inside the front doors, apparently back from a jog. From Wendell's odd viewpoint, it took him a minute to recognize his savior, Alicia. Although sweaty, she looked resplendent in her belly baring shirt and yoga pants.

In a louder voice, she said, "*Why* are you screaming my *name*?"

Wendell shut up, quit wriggling. His captors stopped walking. Wendell dangled between them like a hammock, blood rushing to his head.

"Alicia, oh my God, you've got to help me!" said Wendell. "Please tell these guys you know me! Tell 'em it's all just a misunderstanding and—"

"Um…who *are* you?" Alicia stepped forward. She dropped into a squat, the kind pandering adults do to children. Seriously squinting. "How do you know me?"

"Um…" Frankly, this bugged Wendell more than his current predicament. Still mad at him, playing revenge games. Unbelievable.

"C'mon, Alicia!" Stuck at a sideways angle, he tried on a smile nonetheless. Charm knew no angles. "Fun's fun and all, but it's me. Wendell." Still no recognition in her eyes, a really convincing act. Now closer, bent over, hands on knees. Inspecting him thoroughly. She pushed up her glasses, and shook her head. "Alicia! It's me! Wendell Worthy! We dated a couple months ago and—"

She straightened, tossed her hands up. Mental light bulbs! "Wendell?" Her voice sounded less than confident, unsure. "The guy who…" Hands slapped her sides. Her voice rose, harsh and in command. One of the reasons Wendell'd blown her off. "For God's sake! We only went out *once*. And it *sucked*. *What* are you doing here, Wendell?"

He pretended he wasn't swinging between the men, framed a serious face. "Alicia, I'm sorry I'm even here.

Believe me. But I'm in trouble. Big trouble. You're my last… Ah, would you guys mind putting me down?"

Vincent looked skeptical. He held on, asked Alicia, "Ms. Saunders, is this…*person* a friend of yours? Say the word and we'll do whatever you want." As if to show Wendell who's boss, the men started swinging Wendell high. Nauseatingly so.

"Um, guys, could you not, um—"

"Wendell," said Alicia, "are you in trouble with the police?"

"Noooo…" On the upswing, Wendell's voice vibrated.

"Are drugs involved?"

"Course noooot…"

"Hurt anyone, abuse any—"

"Gahhh! Law-abiding citizennnn!"

"All right guys, put him down," she said.

Clump.

"Ow!" Honestly, when they dropped Wendell, it didn't hurt that much, not compared to his pride. He rubbed the back of his head, glowered at the two men.

"You sure about this, Ms. Saunders?" Hands akimbo, Vincent glowered down at Wendell. "I don't think—"

"It's all right, Vincent." Alicia folded her arms, sighed. "I'm sure I'll regret it, but for now I'll vouch for him."

"As you say, Ms. Saunders." Vincent wiped his hands as if to erase Wendell's taint. "Do get some clothes on him. Management policy."

"I'll see what I can do." She kicked the bottom of Wendell's sneaker. "Well? Get up already! You're embarrassing me." In a hurry, she walked toward the elevator. Finally—finally!—the elevator doors swung open.

Trying to maintain what little dignity Wendell had left, he crawled to his knees, climbed to his feet, raced toward the elevator. The doors whooshed shut as soon as he'd entered.

Leaning back against the mirrored wall, arms still folded, Alicia only had eyes for her phone. Other than the U-2 ballad piped in over the speakers—a brave new world of Muzak, Wendell supposed—they rode in silence.

Finally, Alicia acknowledged Wendell. Looked him up and down, the way he'd been greeted all night. Asked, "You wear tighty-whities?"

First thing on her mind. Typical. Wendell remembered her as being rather self-centered, all talk, talk, talk about herself. About the things she liked and didn't like, clearly the underwear bottoming out her list.

Although not a fan himself, Wendell felt the sudden need to defend his damned tighty-whities.

In a cathartic moment he didn't realize he needed, his words ran away, everything rushed together in a Cliff's Notes version of events.

"I only wore tighty-whities just this once, I was out of laundry, then my brother mouthed off to the local, psychotic drug dealer who kidnapped him and killed a guy, then said he'd kill my brother if I didn't get him chili in my underwear with no help, money or car, then I had to climb a mountain—a friggin' mountain in Missouri!—full of cougars and snakes and poison ivy and hypodermic needles and who knows what else, then I pissed off the homeless and their gang chased me into a church where the priest nearly blew my head off, and the drug dealers' henchmen—that's not racist to say, is it? "Henchmen?"—chased me with a whip onto 14th Street where I had to do the Robot dance—the goddamn *Robot*!—for a bachelorette party, then Vincent tried to bully me and—"

Ding.

The doors whumped open onto the seventh floor. A bare smile—more than he remembered seeing on his date with Alicia and had it really only been one date?—tugged up the corners of her mouth. She walked out. Wendell followed her down the hall. His feet pressed deeply into the carpet, so deep he felt like a kid in a bouncy tent. At the doorway, Alicia whipped out a keycard—from where he couldn't be sure as she appeared to have no pockets, definitely no purse—and opened the door. Before they stepped over the threshold, she furrowed her brow, said, "You did the Robot in your tighty-whities?"

"Gah! Still with the underwear!"

She smiled, sadistically so, as she entered her apartment. Vanished into a room down the hallway.

"Okay! I'm wearing tighty-whities! Get used to it! It's a one-time thing and I swear to God I'll keep up on my laundry from now on!" He paced the apartment, shouting, hoping to be heard. For once. "Everything else I've told you and all you can focus on is my damn underwear? That's so typical! Always about yourself! I—"

"Stop!' Like an enraged genie, she popped out of the hallway, primed to chew him out. She held something wadded up in a fist, but it didn't appear too threatening, possibly a rag. "What the hell's that supposed to mean, Wendell?"

Suddenly feeling quite naked (and he thought he'd pretty much become immune to that feeling by now), he cupped his hands over his crotch. "Um…what?"

"You said I was selfish!" She leaned against the doorjam, waiting.

"I didn't, ah, say that in so many words. What I *said* was—"

"I only care about *myself*."

Damage control to the rescue. The way tonight had gone, he needed a full team of lawyers to get in front of all his problems. "Look, Alicia, I'm sorry you took it that way. I didn't mean anything by it. Just—"

"Yes, you did."

"…you know, we really didn't hit it off on our date, that's all I'm sayin'. So I didn't call you back. Guess the chemistry just wasn't there. Nothing you did, okay?" He served a smile. She lobbed back a glare. The score: definitely not "love-love." "Sorry for blowing you off. But right now, I need—"

"Whoa, whoa, *whoa*!" She moved like a torpedo: fluid, silent and deadly. A finger jabbed the air, perilously close to his eye. "You blew *me* off? *Me*? Listen, dumbass, first of all…" Thankfully, she lowered the deadly digit and struck off a point with it. "…I *never* gave you my phone number! By *choice*!"

"Um…I really don't think that's how things—"

"Oh, yeah? You got my number in your phone? Hell, no! I keep it tight, so I don't get texted day and night by needy—"

"I'm not needy," he muttered and never felt more needy.

"…guys like you! And you think our so-called date was all about *me*? Think again, Romeo! You wouldn't shut up bragging about yourself!"

He couldn't suppress a smile, a condescending one he hoped he disguised well enough. She had a selectively poor memory. "I hardly think that's how it went down." Although come to think of it, he didn't remember getting her phone number.

"Man, listen to you! Here's how it 'went down!'" Her harsh finger quotes could've sliced paper. "You 'member how we met, right?"

"Um… Sure, you—"

Her hand flew up: *halt before I shoot*! "I'll save you the trouble, 'cause no doubt you'll get it wrong. You came into where I work, the Sushi Swan Dive, got hammered. Then built up enough liquid courage to ask me out. I felt sorry for you, thought you were mildly cute…" She held up her thumb and forefinger, an inch apart, and squinted between them to glimpse his minimal cuteness.

"You felt sorry for me?"

"Oh, I'm just getting started! You remember where our date was?"

Not at all. "Of course I do. Ah…only mildly cute?"

"And losing cute ground by the second. You told me to meet you at the Swan Dive. The friggin' place I work!"

Now it came back to him, glimpses fitting together like puzzle pieces. "Hey, I was tryin' to make it easy on you. Besides…I thought you could get an employee discount and—"

"Yeah, I know, big spender. You told me about your plan like it was some brilliant masterstroke I should've fawned over. My girlfriends told me I shouldn't have gone out with you. They said it was a bad idea, some cheap idiot wanting to take me to my workplace—"

"Not an idiot."

"Then *why* are you in those gawd-awful tighty-*whities*?"

"Okay, look, Alicia, clearly you have issues regarding unresolved—"

"Oh my God, if you say 'unresolved romantic feelings,' I swear I'm going to throw you out the window!"

"No, no, no…that's not what I was going to say. Not at all!" Of course it was. But he'd rather not end up as underwear-clad road-kill. "Alicia, I'm sorry about our date. Really." Smoothly rejecting culpability and side-stepping the blame game altogether. "I'm running out of time. We can talk later—"

"What's there to talk about? Just forget it!" Again, her eyes scanned him head to toe. He felt like a side of beef in a butcher shop window. Her head shook, eyes rolled. "Here, put these on." She threw the grey item she'd been holding at him. He flinched, barely snagged it. Sweat pants' legs unrolled to the floor. "You're pretty small," she said. "They're pretty baggy on me. Probably fit you, though. I'll be back in a minute."

"I'm not small," he eeked as she left the room.

He lowered the pants, stepped one foot in, then the other. He shimmied until they tightened at his thighs. With a grunt, he tugged, barely moved them over his hips. The ankles rode high, capris pants high, but they'd do in a pinch. And pinch they did, tightening on his groin to embarrassing effect, no secrets left untold. Worse than the underwear. *Almost*. The material across his butt stretched taut, so tight it'd probably restrict his running speed. He considered making a preemptive tear to loosen up his flexibility—just a small one—but discarded the idea as a bad one. Alicia was already plenty miffed at him. In a mirror, he checked himself out. He looked pathetic, like a geek's first day at the gym wearing his mother's hand-me-downs. On the other hand, it beat tighty-whities.

"I really gotta get going, Alicia!" he called out. "I really appreciate the sweat—"

"Hang on just a minute," she answered.

He looked at the mini grandfather clock over the fireplace mantle—a fireplace, for God's sake!—practically saw time running away from him. Ten-twenty-five. He had one hour, seven minutes left. An invisible noose lowered around his neck, tightened, the perfect fashion accessory for the man-on-the-go. He could still make it by his deadline, only if he didn't waste any more time. Like now.

"You got a car, Alicia?" Just a sudden thought, probably another bad one. He knew it flew against Big Ben's rules. But maybe he could pull it off if he could stay ahead of Ben's guys.

"What? Hell, no! You think I'm rich or something?"

Which is exactly what he thought she was, thought it since he found out where she lived. Her waitress tips must've provided major bank.

Extraordinarily clean and lavish, the apartment had been decorated in a very Euro-chic style. All grays and whites and every imaginable shade between splashed around in big strokes and bigger bucks. The hardwood floor gleamed like a movie star's dental work. A kitchen held more square footage than the entirety of

Wendell's loft; hell, he could move into the kitchen and never get in Alicia's way. The place even had a lounge and a rooftop swimming pool. All this on a waitress's salary. So, yes he did, indeed, think she came from money. Or at least her family did.

Alicia strolled out carrying another garment and a pair of shoes. She caught him picking up a vase, checking the underside for a price-tag. Startled, he nearly dropped it. "Sorry, I was just, ah—"

"It's a knock-off. Whatever." She sat down on her sofa, kicked off her shoes. Slipped into the new pair, made it look easy. Then she tossed him a shirt. "It's the biggest one I have." She shrugged. "Take it or leave it."

He nearly left it. Winnie the Pooh, no pants on, his brother in arms. Strolling, arm around Christopher Robin. Still, any shirt might help deflect unwanted attention.

Always shy—although, frankly, it seemed kind of moot now—Wendell turned away, lassoed the shirt over his torso. The shirt didn't reach his navel. In the mirror, he looked like a Chippendale dancer gone to seed.

"Winnie the Pooh? Really?"

"I like Winnie. Problem with that?" Busy bundling her magenta-dyed hair into a topknot, she glowered at Wendell. On edge, ready to spring off the sofa at the first sign of antagonism. Her blatant anger issues reinforced Wendell's decision not to pursue another date with her.

"No problem. Winnie's awesome. Thanks." Honestly, he couldn't understand why she'd decided to help him. Earlier, he'd just assumed she would—ignorance on his part, he owned—but now her words and actions warred with one another. “Alicia, why are you helping me? I mean…you know…”

She shrugged. Again with that alluring almost, but not quite there, smile. Softening. “I dunno. Really, you kinda don’t deserve it. But…I guess I’m a sucker for a sob story. And, yours? Well…it’s one of the saddest, most pathetic things I’ve ever heard.”

“I aim to inspire sorrow.”

She ignored his sarcasm. “But a lot of your trauma I just don’t get. I want a full recounting. This time done at a non-hyper-freakout speed.”

“Alicia, I don’t really have time to—”

“Shut up, already. Besides… you’re more human now than you were on our date. More vulnerable. You know…” A shrug. “Almost tolerable, I guess.”

This heretofore softer side of Alicia he might have to make time for. At a later date. “I’ll take tolerable, I guess. But I gotta go. I’ll bring back your clothes when—”

Her nose wrinkled. “Ew. Really don’t think I want ’em back. But you wanted my help? You got it. I’m all in now. I have to see how this story turns out.”

“*What*? You’re *not* going with me.”

“And you’re *not* telling me what to do. I’m *going*.” She stood, bounced on her feet. Warming up.

“Oh my God, you don’t get it! These guys are dangerous! If they see you with me, they could do *anything*. I can’t take a chance that—”

“Not *your* chance.” Her eyes rolled, a spectacular performance. “Stop being sexist.”

“I’m *not* sexist.”

“So oinks the pig in the living room. I’m going. Deal with it.” Already in race form, she slow jogged toward the front door. "Coming?"

"Seriously, if they see us together, they might kill my brother. And you and me just for fun."

"They'll never see me. I'm a ghost." Spooky fingers wiggled. "*Ooooooh….*"

Wendell considered it. Mentally, he tabulated an incredibly long laundry list of reasons why she shouldn't come along. Yet the thought of having company for the rest of the journey comforted him. Even if she was combative company. Besides, she wouldn't take no for an answer and he had to go. Push comes to shove, he could always outrun her, leave her behind in his shoe dust.

"Fine. Have it your way. Good luck keeping up with me. I'm fast. I—"

Her eyes shut. She fell against the door, the back of her hand to her forehead as if she had a terrible fever. Wendell freaked, thought she'd suffered a bout of narcolepsy, until she feigned an awful snoring sound. "Heard it all before, Wendell," she said, opening her eyes. "Several times, in fact, on our so-called date. Don't worry about me, Flash. Betcha I can smoke you."

"We'll see." He grinned, hustled to the door. Out of a night of challenges, this one he might enjoy. He swayed an arm, gave a little bow. "Ladies first."

"Sexist much?" Her temporary amusement—flirtation?—vanished. She wrenched open the door and invited Wendell out into the hallway. "None of that crap on my watch."

Wendell took his cue, quickly walked toward the elevators. Inside the elevator, Wendell asked, "Um, any back exits? You know, so I can avoid Vincent?"

She gave him a look, an irritated one, one that

screamed, *Really*?

I think I just made a big mistake…

The elevator doors opened with a hollow *thwump*. Ever vigilant, almost as if expecting them, Vincent stood before the doors. Arms folded in a pissy, prissy manner. He didn't say anything, didn't have to. One eyebrow lifted. His gaze wandered over Wendell's new wardrobe. Apparently too much for him, he walked away, hands on hips, shaking his head, his message clear: *They don't pay me enough for this*.

One foot out the door, Wendell couldn't help himself, said, "Vincent, could you see that my tighty-whities are dry-cleaned by the time we get back?"

Alicia shoved him through the doors, then socked his arm.

"What the hell was *that* for?"

"Really, Wendell? *Really*? If I have to explain it to you, you really are a lost cause."

While stretching, Wendell grumbled, "*Not* a lost cause. My cause is good and just. I'm such a found cause, people turn to me with their causes. *Lost*. Ffft." He took off, weaving around sidewalk dawdlers, marveling at the new relief he felt as he no longer had to hide. He turned back, and said, "I haven't got all day, Alic—"

She'd vanished. Until he heard her. In front of him. Running, looking back over her shoulder, cockier than a weathervane. "So, what're you waiting for?"

He caught up. She glanced over, jerked her chin toward the bubble-wrapped ankle monitor in Wendell's fist. As if she hadn't noticed the elephant in the room before. "That the bracelet?"

"Yep."

"Huh. Just get rid of it."

"Can't." He huffed out a two-fold breath: 1) a runner's cleansing; 2) irritation. "Big Ben's rules say I've got to keep it."

"Still seems to me we'd be better off without it. You always live by others' rules?"

"Whatever," he huffed. Somewhere along the way, some time before his showdown with the homeless, he imagined, the bracelet had finally quit beeping. Hadn't really had time to notice it until now. Still, the red night blinked on, insistent as an ingrown toenail.

They ran down the block, silent. Not in companionable silence, the way Wendell would've preferred it. Rather their voices couldn't be heard over Kansas City unleashed. Revelers bounced from bar to bar, others held court with animated conversation on the decks of coffee houses. The Power and Light district offered the trendiness of Portland, Oregon compacted into a small six block region: cigar bars; a "dry bar (Wendell had no idea what that constituted, but based on the category alone, he wouldn't be visiting);" a "protein house (again, a no-go);" salons, spas and stylists all boasting of "polished" this and that; cookie shops; bakeries; and of course, a couple of gyms to work off the sweets. They rounded the corner, jogged down Main Street through the amassed night wanderers, unable to break away at the speed Wendell needed to. But part of him felt safety in numbers. Now clothed (for better or worse), he welcomed the throng of people, because after all, no one would dare attack him in a crowd. Or so he kept telling himself.

Unfortunately, the crowd thinned the farther they jogged.

"How 'bout telling me your story now," said Alicia. "Without the hyperventilation and hyperbole."

He did, even though it played pretty much like a word-for-word recreation of his earlier recounting. Alicia said nothing, just grinned her Cheshire cat grin, suggesting she had all the answers and wanted to greedily keep them locked up to herself. Really, Wendell expected a little empathy, anything but Alicia's quiet amusement. *Whatever*. He channeled his irritation into his mission, his running. Fuel for his trial by fire.

Once they crossed 13th Street, the storefronts took an immediate nosedive. So did the street life. Sure, there were still a few Power and Light stragglers, those late to the party, those bold enough (or cheap enough) to avoid paying the parking lot fees, risking the potential of parking far away.

They ran far into the dark heart of downtown, the area not yet gentrified or adopted by the young and foolish.

Coffeehouses gave way to tattoo joints. Iron pull-out gates guarded closed pawn shops. *Checks Cashed* screamed the hollow promise emblazoned across several long shuttered store windows. Legs stuck out of darkened, recessed doorways. Wendell had to wonder if these were sleeper agents in the homeless army, laying in wait for Wendell, communicating through carrier pigeons, bats, rats, or however the hell they communicated with one another.

"I don't usually jog this area at night," offered Alicia. "Kinda dangerous."

At the corner of 12th and Main, Wendell stopped, continued jogging in place. He wanted to say, "good to know, Captain Obvious," but held his tongue. His tongue had already stuck him in a lot of unpleasant situations tonight.

Wendell had another reason not to rock the boat. A reason that sort of snuck up on him with the subtlety of a sledge-hammer to the toe. Beneath the moon's soft caress, Alicia looked stunning. Behind her glasses—the ugly, dark-framed, hipster glasses Wendell thought belonged only on '60's sit-com kids—her emerald eyes projected an almost otherworldly cat-like glow. She jogged a circle around him, stopped. Gave him a quizzical look, her lips parted to highlight brilliantly perfect teeth.

"*What?* Now who's wasting time?" She jerked her chin down 12th street. "Little over a mile down that way. Boom. Chili-time."

"Did you really think I sucked? I mean as a date?"

This time when she rolled her eyes, God help him, he found it endearing. "Yes," she said.

Absolutely certain he made a ridiculous sight standing at 12th and Main at night, dressed in a Winnie the Pooh shirt, jogging in place, and primed for a spectacular mugging, Wendell simply didn't care. In fact, for a brief lull, he forgot all about his brother, his task. He wanted to know. *Had* to know. For a second, the harsh, hurried world stopped rotating. Nothing else mattered.

"Why?" he asked. "I mean, why did I suck?"

"I already told you…you kept bragging about yourself." Her shapely legs churned the sidewalk. "Besides my workplace isn't where I—"

"Already explained that."

"We went 'Dutch.'"

"Your choice!"

"Probably," she said. "But it wouldn't have killed you to put up a little fight over the check. The gentlemanly thing to do."

"Now you're saying I'm not a gentleman? When I *try* using manners, you call me sexist! Gah! I can't win!"

"All right, fair enough. But I wouldn't have let you paid for me, anyway. 'Cause I didn't want you sniffing around me again."

"Excuse me? I *don't* sniff."

"True. You slobbered like a horny hound dog. Can't *believe* you tried to kiss me during our crappy date. Where I worked! In front of everyone!"

"I *did*?" Fog swirled around Wendell's recall, slowly lifting. Suddenly the man behind the curtains drew back Wendell's drapes. "Oh my *God*…I *did*, didn't I?" Images tumbled through Wendell's mind, an avalanche of embarrassment: drinking too many beers, clumsily leaning over the table to kiss Alicia, knocking over a lit candle, trying to slap out the flame with his fingertips (which explained the blister he woke up with), other mortifying events that seemed damned charming to him at the time. He wished he could erase it all. "Man, I'm so sorry, Alicia, I—"

"Yeah, pretty damn sorry, all right. Your icky table groping ended our date on a spectacular note."

The memories kept coming, all the happenin' hits. And a few on Alicia, too. "Well… In my defense, I guess I was kinda tossed off-guard by—"

"You mean you were 'on-guard' at some point?" she asked.

"In my defense, you *did* ask, kinda snootily, 'I'll

bet you're a Republican, aren't you?'"

She stopped. Dropped her arms. Surprised, she said, "Did I say that? *Like* that?"

"Yeah, you did."

"Okay, maybe it was wrong of me to assume—"

"And you know what they say when you 'assume'," offered Wendell with a wink. Too soon, story of his life. "It makes an ass out—"

"Don't even go there, 'Grandpa'!" Alicia burrowed back into the trenches of war. "Fine! I shouldn't have asked you about your political beliefs, not like that. But you kept goin' on about my money, asking me about my 'rich' family. How about when you—"

"Sorry, yeah, sorry."

"All those stupid, presumptuous, *rude* money questions, I got the feeling you were some Republican kid, Daddy's boy rebelling, slumming it."

"Not true! Well…maybe I *am* rebelling a little bit, but you—"

"I *knew* it! Then I wondered if you were one of those privileged white kids wanting to go out with me because I'm part Asian. Some kinda pervy, subverted racist kick."

"Wait. *What*? That never even crossed my mind! You don't *get* the right to make that assumption about me! That's *absolutely* not fair! It's—"

"Then why'd you ask me out?"

"I thought you were gorgeous! Funny, intelligent, everything!" He grabbed her shoulders, looked into her eyes. In the movies, it was the moment the hero always smashed his face against the heroine's, and she, in turn, couldn't help but swoon over the male aggression. But the way her nose wrinkled, how her lips switched to one side and stayed there, that incredibly intimidating downturned brow, brought him back down to reality and reminded him he wasn't a movie star. And his script sucked anyway.

Under his grip, her shoulders tensed. Her fists coiled. He released her before she belted him one.

"Okay, sorry I grabbed you, but—"

"Yeah, I've heard nothing but apologies all night from you, Wendell!"

"I only wanted to—"

Vroom. Screeee…

Simultaneously, their heads whipped left. Two blocks West on 12th Street, bright car lights burst from the darkness. Tires screeched, a sound Wendell'd hoped never to hear again. Unmistakable throbbing bass music announced Big Ben's crew coming to pay another visit.

"Your buddies?" asked Alicia.

"'Fraid so." Standing within the shadows of the building next to them, Wendell didn't think Ben's crew could've possibly seen them yet. Just following the ankle monitor's GPS. Eastbound on 12th, traffic appeared nearly nonexistent, but so were hidey-holes. Out of ideas, lost in a strange terrain he didn't know, Wendell froze.

"Come on, dammit!" Alicia grabbed Wendell's hand, wrenched him off the wall. "I got an idea."

Although rather pleasant, holding Alicia's hand under survival circumstances kinda back-burnered Wendell's frustrated romance. He snapped to and released her hand so they could propel more efficiently. Both arms jacking, knees pulling high, they ripped caddy-corner across the intersection of 12th and Main. Behind them, a bus's horn blasted. The large vehicle whooshed by them at a dangerously fast speed, upholding the daredevil reputation of mass transit drivers. The onrush of wind nearly lifted them, pushed them faster.

The Impala's music grew louder. Wendell and Alicia ran down Main toward 11th, avoiding large pools of streetlight.

Brakes locked. Wendell looked back. The Impala ground to a halt within the 12th Street intersection. Horns announced displeasure over Bodacious's traffic blocking move. Undeterred, Bodacious backed up.

Headlights swept up, lowered, straightened into the street as the Impala crept down Main toward them. A flashlight's beam flickered from the car's window, searching. Wendell ducked. Again, Alicia gripped Wendell's hand, said, "This way!" Nearly pulling his arm out of his socket (girl had hidden strengths), she yanked Wendell into a pitch-black alley. Alicia pressed a fingertip to her lips. In a half-squat, she led Wendell half-way down the alley. They hunkered behind a dumpster, a locale where Wendell seemed to be spending too much time lately.

On the street, the Impala's engine slowed, burping along. Little Ben's voice, higher than a kite, hollered, "Come out, Wendy, we know you're here somewhere! Just checkin' up, makin' sure you're honorin' the rules."

Suddenly, the Impala's engine growled. The car pulled up beside the alley. The flashlight's beam found the nook, grazed it, lifted over the dumpster. Wendell gripped the back of the receptacle as if trying to meld with it. Cool, calm even, Alicia didn't flinch. Just chilling, breathing evenly. Like she'd experienced this sort of thing before.

A hushed argument—although loud enough to hear from the alley—broke out amongst Ben's crew.

Jiggy said, "G, I ain't goin' down there. You know I gotta thing about rats."

"Chicken-shit," said Bodacious.

"You go then! See who's chicken-shit."

"Gotta park the car first."

The car pulled past the alley. The engine turned off. So close now, Wendell could hear the engine ticking.

At the opposite end of the alley—so far, far away—freedom waited. So did a streetlight, so glaringly potent it'd illuminate them with targets on their backs.

To their right, a door opened. Rusty hinges cried out. Country music and laughter drifted out before the door snapped shut. A large figure stepped into the glow of the streetlamp. A cigarette dangled from his mouth. He struck a match.

A perfect time for the ankle bracelet to beep again.

Eeep…eeep…eeep…

The man jumped, uttered a string of poetic obscenities. He bent down, squinted at Wendell and Alicia. As if on a Sunday stroll, he sauntered toward them.

His walrus mustache lifted, a friendly how-do-you-do grin. With ruddy red cheeks and a beard that traveled toward his navel, he looked like Santa Claus gone rouge, on holiday as a lumberjack. He proffered a hand toward Wendell, said, "Dunno why you're down there, friend, but you're in the right place."

Puzzled, Wendell accepted the hand, a welcome

change, anything to gain entrance into the building the man had just come from. Suspicion clouded the man's eyes when he helped Alicia up, then the storm passed.

"You brought a lil' friend, huh?" He scratched his beard, smiled, friendliest damn guy since Mister Rogers. "Takes all kinds. Let's get you two inside. The gang's a'waitin'."

Wendell didn't know what gang awaited them, but surely they wouldn't be as dangerous as the gang currently pursuing them. The man moved slowly, reverently, treating Wendell like royalty, ushering him every step of the way. Creeped out, Wendell stepped out of the man's ever-present hand on his back. Together, Wendell and Alicia mounted the back two steps to the door.

Jolly St. LumberNick hurriedly pulled a few final drags from his smoke. "Well, now, glad to see such enthusiasm from you, kid," he said to Wendell. "Last guy we had in here acted like he was bored out of his gourd."

Words like that should've sent warning bells clanging through Wendell. But from around the corner, on Main Street, three car doors slammed. Footsteps followed, one of them kicking a can down the street. Little Ben's girlish laughter. A beam of light bounced across the sidewalk in front of the alley. And Jiggy's damn whip snapped.

Into the unknown Wendell and Alicia leapt. Just inside the narrow hallway, Wendell stopped and attempted to slowly close the door behind them so it didn't slam and give them away. With a large hand, the lumberjack reached in, and stopped the door. He stepped inside, the three of them tightly squeezed into the hallway. The stench of cigarette smoke rolled off the man.

"I'm Dale by the way," he said with a holiday chortle. "Hey, like your shirt." He tapped Wendell's Pooh garment. "Very appropriate for the occasion."

"Wait…what—"

Dale shoved Wendell down the hallway, Alicia tagging closely behind. Wendell's sneakers stuck to the wooden floor, then released with a sticky-sounding *squelch.* They passed a bathroom door, cleverly marked "bathroom," the establishment forward thinking in utilizing a uni-sex facility. Music welcomed them: warbling, yodeling, heartbroken lyrics about love gone wrong, a bullet gone right, and a pick-up truck more faithful than a woman. All the sounds of a bar in fine form: laughter, good-natured razzing, glasses clinking and chunking down onto tables, the vocal buzz of a community bonding in the town hall of alcohol.

Dale's palm returned to Wendell's back, his fingers into his shoulder. He steered him around the corner and into the bar.

First thing Wendell noticed: they'd definitely left Trend Town behind. Nearly saloon style, the bar could've been magically transported from out of the Old West. Poorly lit, ancient neon beer signs behind the bar lent an unhealthy jaundice to the digs. Ancient lamps, complete with cobwebs grown to artistic proportions, hung over shoddy wooden booths. First bar Wendell'd ever seen that didn't have at least one big-screen TV monopolizing the wall. A small, quaint, barely elevated dance floor—not much more than 12' by 12'—anchored the far end next to the jukebox. Everything was, indeed, *not* up-to-date in Kansas City.

The alarming number of patrons who resembled Dale scored second on the "Things Wendell Noticed" list. Awash in a sea of flannel and jeans, the crowd must've flocked here after a woodworker's convention or something. Orange, red, and brown fringed beards looked like Fall had really let itself go. A few other, younger men sat at some of the tables, a couple at the bar, always deeply embroiled in conversation with a lumberjack or two. Upon seeing Wendell, the men stopped talking.

Uh-oh.

Alicia grabbed the back of Wendell's shirt, tugging it, trying to get his attention.

"Look who I found in the alley, boys," shouted Dale. "Welcome to the Bear Hole!" He slapped Wendell's back, edging him into a table. The table wobbled. Beer sloshed over a pitcher's edge. The seated men stared at their spilled beer. Prepared for a pummeling, Wendell backed up and bumped into Dale's voluminous belly. Huge grins peeked out from beneath the men's beards. Cheers and applause rode around the bar.

Really uh-oh.

A distressing lack of women in the bar was the third thing Wendell noticed and he kicked himself for not realizing that first.

Beyond uh-oh.

Behind the bar, the words, *The Bear Hole,* were emblazoned at the top of the room-length mirror. Next to the legend, a caricature of a large bear, tongue lolling out in a disturbing manner, cradled a small cub with its paw. Entering the realm of self-consciousness once again, Wendell rolled up the image of Winnie and

Christopher on his shirt. Then he realized his nipples were exposed, probably a worse idea, and lowered the curtain again. More applause met this embarrassing move.

Definitely straight out of a western flick, the bartender leaned across the bar. Red eyebrows lifted. He sat down a mug he'd been polishing with a bar towel. When he spoke, the tips of his handlebar mustache fluttered.

"'Bout damn time," he said. "Boys were gettin restless."

"Um, I really think there's been a mistake here. I—"

"Hey, we been waitin' over an hour now!" Dale gripped Wendell's arm and maneuvered him through the crowd. "I knew we shouldn't've paid up front!"

Helpless, Wendell looked behind him, hoping for Alicia's assistance. To his astonishment, she'd bellied up to the bar, full mug in hand. She gave Wendell a little wave.

How much is she gonna make me pay for one stupid date?

Dale snatched the wrapped bracelet from Wendell's hand. A puzzled look on his face, he turned it over and studied it. "What's this for? A beeper? You don't need a beeper. You're contracted here for an hour."

"No, wait! It's not a beeper! And I'm not—"

"More action, less talk!" Dale slapped Wendell's back again, clearly not realizing his own bear strength. Wendell stumbled. "And unless this is a tambourine or something, you ain't gonna need it for what you're about to do!" At the closest table, Dale dropped the bracelet into a full pitcher. Wendell watched it sink, taking his hope down with it.

"Nooo! You don't understand! I need—"

"Come on now, son…" Talking like he was Wendell's father now, for crying out loud, as if the endless night of torture wasn't about to get far worse. "Lookie…your beeper's still blinking." Dale tapped the pitcher. Sure enough, the damn bracelet seemed indestructible, built out of cockroach carcasses or something. The red light blinked off and on. Frankly, Wendell would welcome the parole officer with open arms right about now. *Anything*.

The crowd's excitement reached a feverish pitch. Cheers. Whistles, the two fingered in the mouth kind only big, burly men mastered. Boots clomped on the wooden floor. Flanneled arms lifted, not unlike the bachelorette party from earlier. Hands cupped around mouths, demanding mush-mouthed, garbled, indecipherable, unintelligible things that could only be sexual acts.

And, just a matter of hours ago, all he'd wanted was a nice, quiet evening with his brother, maybe a few beers, maybe—hopefully—get a phone number from a lovely lady.

Wendell's chances of that happening now seemed on the down side of never.

"Go on, boy," urged Dale. "Get up on stage. Show the fellas what you got!" Numb from inescapable terror, Wendell tripped on the single step up. He regained his balance, and turned around on the stage. Strapped to the ceiling, only a foot-and-a-half above him, small floodlights snapped on. Wendell's arm went up, shading his eyes. When he looked out over the rowdy crowd, all he saw were round, big bear silhouettes, but mostly, glaring lights.

"Hit the music, Kevin," called out Dale.

Kevin—a dark figure hunched over the jukebox machine, Quasimodo in his bell-tower—tapped away at the buttons with the fluidity of a pianist.

Music swelled. Loud and thrumming, vibrating the dance floor. The senseless notes wormed up into Wendell's bowels, stirring a queasy soup. Several lines of the song played out before he recognized the tune: *YMCA* by the Village People.

Although the music pumped out at ear-rending decibels, the men's enthusiasm dampened. The cheering stopped. Shadowy shapes of heads bobbed back and forth, blending together into a multi-headed beast of secret, sexual conspiracy. Just waiting for the unimaginable ritual to begin.

Someone yelled, "You gonna dance or what?"

Crap.

Wendell felt like an idiot. An extremely relieved idiot, but he'd take it.

Fine, all they want is a dance or two, I'll give them that, no harm, no foul, fastest way to be on the road again lickety-split.

For a guy who couldn't dance for his life, it was the second time tonight his life depended on his dancing non-skills, though. But, honestly, he doubted the guys really cared about dance moves.

If I survive this, my brother's gonna pay!

"Move yer ass, sweet thang!"

Immediately, Wendell ruled out "The Robot." He thought robots and bears might be natural enemies. He reached deep into his catalog of American Bandstand

TV recollections, pulled out what he could remember about the infamous Village People song, blew dust off it.

He hopped, landing with his legs apart. Arms up, forming a "Y."

A few claps, not much. Tough crowd. Surely, he could do better. Elbows extended, shoulders back, his version of an "M." "C" proved easiest, one arm above and over, the other under. For "A," he put himself in mind of a Christmas tree, hands together above his head, legs straddled.

"It's fun to stay at the Yyyy, M, C, A-ayyy…"

After his first formation of the song's title, several of the men clapped. Whistled. Somewhat of a better response. He duplicated the move. One more time. Damn song repeated the refrain about a thousand times. But at least he'd mastered it. Easy-peasy. Wash, rinse, repeat…

Jesus, how long is this song?

"It's fun to stay at the Yyyy, M, C, A-ayyy…"

Appreciation stepped aside for unrest. His audience grew fidgety. Heads shook. The boo's hurt the most. He had to give the guys something more, one riot a night his limit.

"Young man, are you listening to me?…"

His faded memories couldn't recall any particular dance moves for the song verses. Just the body formation of the letters performed en masse, sort of a Sesame Street for adults.

Driving the song, though, beneath the flashy vocals and pyrotechnical disco, he heard—*felt*—a sort of military band march theme, something he could work with. He drew upon his aborted two weeks in the high school ROTC program.

"I said, young man, put your pride on the shelfff…"

He pulled his knees up as high as the sweats would allow him, not nearly the perfect horizontal lines he'd aimed for. One leg after the other, arms pumping in a sort of slow run movement. He turned in a circle, marching in place. Military style. Kept going, round and round and…

"Booo!"

"Do something, dammit!"

"That all you got? I seen fish in a bowl that're more excitin'!"

The natives grew agitated, edgy. A change of pace, then.

Wendell abandoned the military groove. He swiveled his hips, not that he had much to swivel, really, a life-long obsession with running saw to that. His audience responded favorably, quieter at least. Soon, he entered the zone, tamed the beat. He faced left, hips gyrating like Elvis, arms swinging up and down. He jumped up, twisted in the air, and landed facing right. Same move, more funk. He channeled Elvis, felt they had a lot in common, his hips really moving now. His arms rocked back and forth perfectly attuned to the rhythm. Boldly, he embellished it with finger snaps. A sassy touch, he wiggled his head around like his neck couldn't support it. Topped it with a few coy smiles: *Who me?*

More cat-calls flung toward Wendell, this time not of the appreciative sort. Rude demands for his removal.

Wendell responded by bringing all of the funk he could muster. Granted, growing up around wealthy, privileged, white bankers probably didn't amount to much funk, but he gave it his all. He spun like a demon possessed him. Shoulders wagged—kudos to Ann Margaret—as he shimmied as close to the floor as possible without falling. Eyes shut, being the beat…

"You can hang out with all the boys…"

And he had to wonder: *Why in hell am I doing this? Even getting into it a little. I need to be saving my brother's worthless ass.*

Then he spotted Alicia and he knew the answer. It wasn't the men he wanted to impress (although a little show of gratitude for his efforts would be nice). Alicia had moved closer to the stage. Sitting at the end of the bar, nursing a beer. Next to her, a neon sign flickered, coloring her green, then dropping her in shadows and back again. Vibrant life and shades of darkness, her two personas. Both of them immensely intriguing.

Wendell focused on her, forgetting his paying audience. She grinned. One leg crossed over the other. A foot tapped out the beat.

Plain and simple, he wanted to impress her.

"Take it off, dammit!" Then the boys pulled him down off his cloud.

"This ain't what we paid to see!"

"Get yer goddamn clothes off, pretty boy!"

Uh-oh, revisited.

Wendell didn't particularly fancy a strip-tease performance. Hell, he'd just got these clothes, crappy as they were. Didn't think much of losing them again.

Some guy banged a pitcher on the table, always an agent provocateur in the crowd. Another man stood, picked up his chair, and pounded it onto the floor. One step away from inciting a riot of angry bears. Wendell knew better than to poke one bear, let alone a bar full of them.

On the other hand, he had his pride to contend with. Something he wanted to show Alicia he had in buckets. A strip-tease prompted by bullying probably wouldn't win her admittedly ice-cold heart.

But something zipped over Wendell's head, and smacked into the back wall. Definitely motivational. And his audience *did* call him a "pretty boy," after all, something he'd never heard before regardless of sexual preference.

In show business, the adage goes: *Give the people what they want.*

Off came the Pooh shirt. He swung the shirt above his head, treating it like a lasso and supplying the requisite "whoops" and "hee-yah's." The song finally, mercifully, ended.

Then things got worse.

A ruckus—louder than the commotion Wendell stirred—arose in the back. The Pooh shirt dropped to his feet.

Three figures stepped out of the back hallway, arms waving, voices yelling. He didn't have to make out the faces to know who they were. Little Ben's wail of a voice made Wendell's cavities hurt.

Several of the bar regulars moved toward Ben's men, waylaying their progress. But Wendell had to move fast.

He didn't want to do it—last thing he wanted to do, but he couldn't let Big Ben's cronies see him in clothes. One leg extended across the floor, duckwalking like Chuck Berry with his guitar, he scraped the sweats off over his shoes, then kicked them into the crowd.

The crowd went berserk. Men scrambled for the sweats, no one wanting them more than Wendell. Sadly, he bid them adieu (*nice knowing you, pants, your valiant sacrifice won't be forgotten*).

A jumble of noisy confusion stirred in the back, Ben's guys acting big, talking even bigger. Wendell spotted a gun waving above the sea of heads. He hopped off the stage, blending into the crowd. Pushing aside beer guts, muscular arms, and shoulders as square as a recliner back, he fought to get to Alicia.

"Goddamn, man, get your faggy hands offa' me!" Little Ben making friends and winning influence. Clearly offended, more men joined the fracas in the back.

A hand latched onto Wendell's arm. Startled, he yelped, but thankfully it went unheard over the shouting. Alicia pulled him toward the back wall, next to her, out of the madness.

Bang!

A gunshot. Overhead lights snapped on. Jiggy brandished a pistol above him, the tip smoking. Old-school western style, it stopped the bar brawl from escalating. The bear gang stood their ground, some shaking their heads, probably wondering how their night had turned. Gone into hibernation.

The bartender looked shifty, pretty much the only look he had. Not so covertly, his hand moved beneath the bar.

Long past time to beat feet the hell outta there.

"Now, lissen up, friends of Dorothy," shrieked Little Ben, "I know lil' red-headed Wendy's in here. You wanna show me where he's at? Before Jiggy here starts perforatin' your flannel?"

"I'll perforate 'em real good, G," said Jiggy.

A lousy magician, the bartender lowered, disappeared in plain sight. Sprung back up, loaded with a shotgun. "Not in my bar, asshole!"

Ka-blam!

The cigarette machine behind Little Ben exploded. Cigarette packages rained down.

"Goddamn!" Little Ben tore back down the rabbit hole in which he'd popped out from.

Jiggy and Bodacious had their guns out, swinging them around, holding the bears at bay while they backed up to follow Little Ben.

Ka-chak!

The bartender cracked his shotgun, and fumbled to plug another shell into it. "Show you to mess with me!"

In a crouch, Wendell and Alicia waddled toward the front door. Wendell reached for the door knob, hoped the bell above it wouldn't draw attention.

The door slammed open. The bell jangled.

Wendell retracted his hand. Not quick enough. The door struck several fingers, jamming his middle finger, the most expressive one. With his other hand, he grabbed the door knob and held the door open. He and Alicia took cover behind it.

The big parole cop, Dayton Bookes, walked in. Stopped. Bringing another gun to the party.

"What the hell's goin' on in here that I *want* to know about and that I *don't* want to know about?" he shouted. "Start with the wants."

Gun out, the other hand providing an ineffective flesh shield in front of him, he slowly walked toward the bartender. Wendell continued holding the door open. Alicia grabbed his hand, the one with the sprained finger. He winced, bit his tongue to keep from grunting. In the shadows, Alicia's eyes were dark, non-existent, but her nod relayed the urgent message clearly: *Now or never.*

"I'm police, dammit!" yelled Bookes. "And I'm *really* gettin' tired of walkin' into gunfights tonight. Don't get me goin' about how damn hungry I am!"

Before they ended up on Bookes' dinner plate, Wendell and Alicia scurried around the door, and practically crawled out onto the sidewalk. One hand on the doorknob, the other guiding the door to soften the bell's ring, Wendell closed it quietly.

And they ran.

****

10:52 P.M.

Upon entering the Bear Hole, Dayton Bookes rolled his eyes, pulled his gun, and demanded everyone's attention. It didn't bother him the Bear Hole was a gay bar; all the cops in KCMO knew it was, and usually it stayed out of the limelight which suited the boys in blue just fine.

What bothered him was the mess he'd either interrupted or was about to get caught in the crossfire from.

The bar's burly patrons stood willy-nilly around the dive. Chairs lay on their backs. Two guys stopped their game of tug-of-war over sweat pants, for God's sake.

The hell's goin' on tonight?

A burnt powder odor hung around like an unwelcome houseguest, the acrid smell that's impossible to mistake for cigarette smoke (not that anyone can smoke in bars anymore, anyway). The sight of the bartender hefting a shotgun didn't exactly give Dayton the warm fuzzies, either. All of it really made Dayton want to toss his hands up, holster his gun, go belly deep at the bar and get three fingers thick into the whiskey.

His stomach grumbled again, reminding him there were more important things to do than drink.

"Put the damn gun down and talk to me. I'm officer Dayton Bookes. What're you called?"

"Wally." Unlike the priest from earlier, Wally complied right away and stashed the gun. Nodded toward the back of the bar. "Fully licensed and everything, Bookes. Don't reckon I need the gun now, though. Guys causin' trouble took off."

Dayton looked toward the back, saw nothing out of the ordinary. Just a lot of big men cordially getting their gay on, although a few had taken to gathering scattered cigarette packs and stuffing them into their flannel shirt pockets.

"Sure they're gone?" asked Dayton.

"Course I am. We don't get many kinds like them in here. Um, no offense."

"By that, you mean they're black?"

"Well, yeah…" Wally looked down, ashamed. "But not only that. I mean, they was skinny, young loud-mouths. Not my usual customer. And they all brought guns, against policy. One of 'em shot his gun."

"That right? Anyone hurt?" Dayton holstered his gun. Business had resumed at the Bear Hole. Chairs were righted, hands shook, apparently a pact to share the sweat pants agreed upon.

"Nah, think he shot up at the roof. You know, I was just protectin' my place, Bookes. And my guys."

"Not after you, Wally." Dayton pulled out his favorite photo, the one he'd been holding lately near and dear to his heart. He nudged the front-facing mug shot across the bar top, hoping for a nibble. "This one of the guys playing gangster?"

Wally leaned across. Instead of picking the photo up, he flattened his hands, lowered his head so his nose nearly touched the picture. "Nope. At least, I don't think so. One of the guys was short and loud-mouthed. One of 'em had a lazy eye. Saw it when I turned on the lights. Hard to miss."

"Uh-huh." Dayton didn't know the men by name, not their real names, but Wally's description fit two of Benjamin Landers' subordinates. "Any of 'em mention Benjamin Landers? Or Big Ben?" Dayton grimaced at the thought of using Landers' stupid "gangsta" name.

"Not that I know. Hey, Buzz! Buzz!"

A guy moseyed over looking anything besides a "Buzz." Hair down to his shoulders, permed, teased and absolutely fried, kinda like his demeanor. His open shirt revealed a raccoon tail of hair down his chest. "Yeah? What's up?"

"You were goin' one on one with the colored…um, black guys, right?" Wally shifted nervous eyes away from Buzz to glance at Dayton. Make sure he hadn't upset the civil rights cart. Dayton just sighed, nodding his head. Nothing he hadn't heard before.

"Guess so," said Buzz.

"The hell were they doin' in here?" asked Dayton.

"Besides causin' shit, I think they were lookin' for our dancer."

"Dancer? First I'm hearin' about a dancer," said Dayton.

"Yeah, skinny-ass kid. He—"

"Don't tell me. Red-head. Strawberry in tighty-whities, right?"

Both Wally and Buzz smiled, momentarily lost in good times. "That's right," said Wally.

This just gets more and more interesting.

"They say what they wanted him for?"

"Nah. Just that they were looking for him."

"What happened to the Strawberry?"

Looking dumber than Buzz probably intended, a shrug pitched up. "Beats me. He kinda vanished when you came in. Can I go now?" Like Buzz had somewhere better to be.

"Yeah, run along," said Dayton. "Be good to one another." Back to Wally, "Any these guys wearin' an ankle bracelet?"

Wally threw his towel over a shoulder, the better to toss both hands up. "When someone's holdin' a gun on you, you don't really look at their ankles, know what I'm sayin'?"

"That I do, Wally." Dayton studied the bar, looking for a menu, pretzels, anything. "Got anything to eat?"

Proudly, with a smile, Wally brought up a mug full of hard-boiled eggs. Maybe just a trick of the crummy lighting, but several of the eggs held a distinctly green tint to them. And it wasn't Easter. Real or imagined, Dayton thought he smelled the odor of sulfur, saw cartoon fumes rolling off the eggs.

Dayton pulled out his phone, looked at the blank screen, bugged his eyes, and said, "Damn, Wally, maybe another time. Gotta go."

Dayton left the bar, checking the GPS on his phone while walking toward his car. Multi-tasking, the way he did all his policing. His ex-wife used to call it “half-assing,” but Dayton preferred the busier sounding of the two options.

On the move again, the green dot headed East on 11th Street, quickly approaching Walnut. Whoever he was—and Dayton strongly suspected the Strawberry—the kid could move. He also seemed invisible, impossible to find, leaving behind a wake of crap.

Dayton cursed at the sight of the new ticket flapping beneath his windshield wiper, plucked it out, scrunched it into his jacket pocket to join its fellow forgotten scraps. He backed off the sidewalk, had second thoughts and chunked it into “Park” again.

He didn’t have time to pay his good friend, Benjamin Landers, a visit. Right now, he wanted the Strawberry badly, suspected if he sweat the kid hard enough, he’d roll over and implicate Landers in something hinky. But Dayton sure as hell could give Landers a call. Catch up a little bit. Feel him out. Squeeze him ‘til he bled.

As if expecting Bookes’ call, Landers answered on the first ring. “Yo, you got Big Ben. Speak.”

Dayton hated the confidence in Landers’ voice; the bull-headed balls or just plain stupidity that fed his sense of invulnerability. In a way, Dayton could almost understand: so far, the justice system had let Landers skate by many times with only a slap on the wrist. Of course, he believed he was Superman. But Dayton wanted to be Landers’ kryptonite, his Lex Luthor. Gotta have goals, he thought. Makes the job interesting.

“Cut the ‘Big Ben’ shit, Benji. Only thing big ’bout you’s your mouth.” Dayton, trying to stir him up a bit.

“Five-O! You miss me or somethin’? Need a hug?”

"Lessee how you like all those hugs you'll be gettin' in prison."

"Shiiit. Now you're just frontin'. Whatchu' want, fat man?"

Fat man? Fat? Damn, more like solid muscle. Maybe a little padding. Doesn't matter. He's just tryin' to turn it around. Tryin' to get to me.

"Much as I know you love flirtin' with me, Benji, what the hell's up with your ankle bracelet? You know it's a crime to tamper with your monitor, right?"

"Man, I meant to tell you! Slipped my mind like alla them discs in your back. You really should lose some—"

"You home?"

"Course I am! I'm a law-abidin' citizen."

"I pay you a visit, you're gonna be waitin' for me?"

"Open arms, G."

"So…where's your monitor then? If you're home, why aren't you wearin' it?"

"That's what I'm sayin'! You know that red-headed cream-puff? One was sittin' in my crib earlier?"

"Don't know him. What's his name?"

"Wendell Worthy."

Dayton switched hands, scribbled the name in a notepad. "What about him?"

"Dude went crazy, Bookes! Clocked me from behind when I wasn't lookin'!"

"Uh-huh."

"That's how it went down. While I'm out, he takes it off me. I wake up. Big headache. No monitor. Dayum, guess the guy's hard-up for some drug money or somethin', know what I'm sayin'?"

"Hardly understand you half the time, Benjamin."

"Well, first he comes lookin' for drugs. I say, 'Man, step off. I'm a clean, law—"

"'Abiding citizen.' Yeah. Move on with the rest of your fairy tale."

"Gospel! So dude cold-cocks me, wham! When I wasn't lookin', did I say already? Used a gun or somethin'. Guess he's gonna pawn the monitor."

"You and me both know that's bullshit, Benji."

"No lie. Got great respect." Dayton heard two hollow thumps, beating his chest, probably kissing the sky next.

"No doubt. So why didn't you call me?"

"Honestly, G, I—"

"Don't call me 'G.'"

"G, it's like this, I didn't wanna get in trouble, you always bustin' my balls and everything. Just trying to be an upstanding citizen now. Do my civic duty and alla that shit."

"Right. Why're your boys shootin' up the neighborhood lookin' for the Strawberry?"

"Don't know nothin' 'bout that. See, in keepin' to the law, I stayed put, snug as a bug and alla that. But I sent my trusted aides out, tryin' to bring lil' Wendy back to justice. Win-win, 'specially for the side of right. If they did somethin', they acted as independent agents. Not my call, G."

Imagining Landers smiling through his gold-capped teeth damn near burnt an ulcer through Dayton's stomach. "I'm gonna find the kid, Benji. When I do, I'm comin' for you."

"Bring flowers, G." Laughing like a Bond villain, Landers hung up.

Dayton added a couple new dents to his glove box. Breathing shallowly and quickly, he switched his phone over to the GPS. Got a current hit on the kid.

The Taurus bumped against the curb, wheeled backward. Headlights shot through Dayton's rear window. The clown behind Dayton switched to bright, and blasted his horn.

"Yeah, yeah, yeah." Dayton stuck his hand out the window, and waved. Took his sweet time adjusting his rearview mirror, humming. Teaching the impatient guy a lesson. Everyone just needed to slow down a little bit in life, smell the flowers and all.

Dayton buzzed the Taurus up the street. "All right, Strawberry," he said, "let's see what patch you're hidin' in."

Chapter Seven

10:53 P.M.

Side by side, Wendell and Alicia raced down 11th Street. A half a block down, a horrific realization struck Wendell.

"Dammit! The bracelet! I gotta go—"

"Chill, dancing machine." Alicia smiled. Held up the dripping wet bracelet. "Got your back."

"*Man*. You saved my life."

As he reached for it, she yanked it back. "Maybe I better hold on to it for a while."

Tired of fighting, Wendell surrendered. "Fine. But don't get separated. I guess they make these things beer-proofed, huh?" He bounced into a slow trot, warming up.

"Probably not the first time someone put one of these to the beer test."

"I don't suppose you grabbed the sweatpants by chance."

Her lip curled up, half smile, all sarcasm. "You kiddin' me? I'm not getting between two guys and a stripper's pants."

He laughed. "I totally owned the stage, right?"

She didn't just laugh, she guffawed. "Right. Keep tellin' yourself that. My God, I've seen better moves in Godzilla movies. I'm talkin' about the monsters—"

"Yeah, I got it. Dancing's not all that tough," he groused. "My cousin, Zach's a dancer with the Kansas City Ballet. If he can do it, anybody can." More than willing to change the subject, Wendell asked her the time.

Alicia consulted her phone. "10:54…no, 10:55."

"Dammit. We're running out of time. We really gotta pick it up here on out. Or we won't make it."

"Fine by me," she said. "No more gay bar visits for you, though."

"Hope not." This time they shared a laugh, first one of the night, probably ever. A pleasant change.

At the corner of 11th and Walnut, Wendell paused, looked down the road, then right, weighing his options. "Think we should go back to 12th? We'll make better time if we go the straight shot. Besides Ben's guys probably think we'll stay on 11th."

"They can track us. Duh." She held up the bracelet as irrefutable proof.

"We outrun 'em. I'm up to it. Are you?"

"You gotta ask? 12th is more crowded than 11th from the looks of things, though. And you're back in your tighty—"

"Underwear, dammit! I thought tighty-whities was just a term kids threw around on the playground."

"Well, it's when boys should *definitely* quit wearin' 'em. Grade school. Just sayin'."

"Can we *please* quit talking about my underwear already? Bad enough everybody in Kansas City's seen 'em. You can help me burn them when we're done with this mess." End of discussion, Wendell ran across Walnut. "We'll stay on 11th then. Just keep an eye open for that damn Impala."

Alicia ran after him. "Don't need open eyes. We can hear it comin' a mile away."

Not only was 11th Street less traveled than 12th, civilization pretty much ceased to exist. At least as Wendell knew and preferred it. Homeless people squatted in abandoned storefront doors. Wendell and Alicia leaped over a series of outstretched legs, one hurdle after the other, taking eggshell caution so as not to incite another riot. Even questionable stores of questionable nature had given up the idea of mercantilism in this ghost land, gone or burnt out of business. Shuttered and barred windows held an ominous aura, menacing eyes in forsaken buildings. Just like the buildings, traffic also had died. Wendell's footfalls sounded like claps of thunder in the unnerving quiet.

He had to break the silence, pull out of the creepy sound-proofed vacuum surrounding him. "So…did I, ah, tell you about the book I'm writing?"

She grinned. Probably not the greatest literary compliment. "Yeah. What's it called? *Pocketful of Lint* or something?"

"Okay… *A Pocketful of Heart*. But you knew that already."

She sniggered, not a good sound for her. "My title's less pretentious."

He slowed, nearly stopped. Ready to straighten her out. "Pretentious? My book's *not*—watch it! Legs!" Without losing stride, they hopped over a pair of outstretched limbs. "My book's *not* pretentious!"

"Yeah, right. You know how many would-be writers—"

"Not 'would-be.' I *am* an author."

She sighed, dropping her voice down a notch. The better to deliver a bombshell, no doubt. "Whatever. Seems like every writer wants to write a book about a starry-eyed writer who wants to write…" She jagged out harsh finger quotes. "…the Great American Novel. Little, sensitive guy trying to make it big in the harsh literary world. You know how often that's been done? How pretentious it all is? Besides…who wants to *read* about writing? It's about as exciting as…reading about laundry or something."

"Wow. Tell me how you really feel, Alicia."

Not that he meant it, but she certainly rose to the challenge. "Fine. Let's look at the facts… You say you're a writer. But you're a waiter."

"That's just temporary. I—"

"Bla, bla, bla. How far have you gotten into *A Fistful of Heart*?"

"*Pocketful*! And, ah… I'm still working on the first chapter."

"Huh. Imagine that. *Watch it*! Trash can!" Shoved along by a sudden gust of wind, the metal can rolled in front of them, off the sidewalk, and into the street. "Why do you 'spose that is? That you haven't made any progress beyond the first chapter?"

"I… Well, I've been pretty busy."

"Welcome to Denial City. Maybe it's 'cause you don't know what you're writing about."

"*What*? Writing's all I know! It's what I'm living! You can't—"

"Simmah down, Wendell. I'm just floatin' this out there. Maybe it's 'cause you haven't really lived life yet."

Tonight, everyone wanted to jump into the literary

criticism arena. But Wendell'd go down fighting over this battle. Even with time dwindling away, he stopped. Hard to present a solid case while running. "You don't know anything about my life, Alicia."

Alicia slowed, and turned around. She ran in place, facing him. "Oh, *really?* Pretty much learned everything about you on our miserable date. *Everything*. Let's see… You grew up in a small town in Kansas, mostly a farming community. Your moneyed family pretty much ruled the town. First your grandfather, then your father owned the bank. Daddy wanted you to follow suit. You rebelled. Came to Kansas City—and, really, shouldn't you be in New York or something?—to strike it big with literary acclaim, fame and fortune. By writing a book about a guy writing a book. And, I'm telling you, it's been done a kazillion times." Finally, she stopped jogging. "What else did you tell me? Oh, your daddy more or less cut you off financially when you insisted on playing out the writer thing. Let's see… Your parents always favored your big brother, the one being groomed for future small town bank supremacy. The idiot who got you into this mess in the first place."

"Ouch. I told you *all* of that?" Deflated, damn near mentally castrated, Wendell rubbed the back of his neck, not much more to say. What could he say? Hard to believe he'd been harboring feelings for her earlier.

"Oh yeah. And tons more. And you still don't know a damn thing about me."

"That's *sooo* not true! You're a waitress at the Sushi Swan Dive and you're beautiful and—"

"You gonna kiss her or *what?*" Wendell jumped, looked around for the voice's owner. From a doorway, a homeless man unfolded his legs. "G'wan, do it, kid! You know you want to!"

"Pshh, yeah, right!" Alicia whirled, hands on hips. "Last thing I wanna *ever* do! *You* got a better chance of mackin' on me than Wendell does!"

"Best offer I had all night, girly!" The man's legs withdrew. His hands clawed the sidewalk as he got up on his knees, then finagled to his feet. His lips puckered, his face a prune. Arms out, coming for some loving.

"Uh, we better get going," said Wendell.

"Good idea."

They sped off, leaving the lovelorn man calling after them. Despite everything going on, Wendell laughed.

"Oh, so *that* you find funny," said Alicia.

"Kinda. So…regardless of the fact you think so little of me, I—"

"Whatever, Wendell. You're just frustrating, that's all."

Based on old movie dialogue, Wendell knew "frustrating" could be as promising as "sexy" or "intriguing." Or it could be taken at face value, a very sour face Alicia seemed hell-bent on wearing. Maybe he did need to face certain facts. "Okay, first of all… You pretty much think my life's boring. Let's hear about yours."

"Why? So you can make fun of me?"

"Well…what's good for the goose and all. But, no…I genuinely want to know about your life." Approaching the intersection of 11th and Grand, they slowed. "Tell me about yourself, Alicia."

She smiled, more like an anti-grimace, but baby-steps. "Well, contrary to what you think, I'm not rich. Neither are my parents. I was adopted. Don't know anything about my biological parents—*Car!*"

They jumped into a door nook, facing one another. Close, very close. A warm plume of her breath caressed his naked chest. Shadows pooled around her eyes, enhancing her with a patina of mystery. Her lips parted with a slight pop, glistening beneath the moonlight. Never very good at timing, particularly when it came to women, Wendell wondered what those lips would feel like on his.

"My parents had to work hard and they did it for me, you know," she said. "Dad was a hospital janitor, which meant long hours and even grosser jobs. Mom worked in my school's cafeteria 'til she got laid off."

"Really?"

"Really, really…shhh."

The car rumbled by. Motor low and threatening. Rap music beating down the trunk. Most assuredly Little Ben and crew. Wendell sucked in his gut, held his breath. Slowly the car ambled down the street and out-of-sight, the boys apparently puzzled by Wendell's no-show. Frankly, he didn't mind the cozy confines of the nook, not one bit. Not this close to Alicia.

"I'm sorry your parents had it rough. They sound like good people."

She nodded, and looked off into the distance, thoughtful.

"But…how can you afford your apartment?" he asked. "It's gotta cost—"

"Shush. Give me a chance to tell my story." She pressed a finger over Wendell's lips. He stood rapt, mesmerized. She grinned, her teeth incandescent.

"I'm not just a waitress, Wendell. I might've got around to telling you that on our date if you would've ever shut up."

"Sorry, sorry, a million times—"

"Actions speak louder than words." Her finger still in place, she bore down harder on his lips. Teasing him, totally owning the lead in their slow dance.

"I got an art scholarship at the Kansas City Art Institute. Full ride."

"Wow. I mean, I had no idea…"

"Of course you didn't. Duh."

Even though the car had long passed, even though time passed quicker, Wendell knew he needed to be in the nook right there, right now. "So…the school's paying for your digs? Your luxury apartment? The one with the swimming pool on the—"

"Dammit, Wendell, you're showing your Republican roots again."

"Totally not fair."

"All's fair in…" She didn't finish the sentence. As much as Wendell wanted her to. "Anyway, shut up for once. *My* story." Wendell nodded, attentive student at teacher's mercy. "Course they wouldn't pay for the Power and Light apartment. My dad did. He insisted. 'Nothing but the best for my lil' girl,' he said. I told him to put his cash away. I knew they couldn't afford it. But he wouldn't take no for an answer. Said he'd been saving his whole life to help me out. I saw it'd hurt him more if I didn't take it. So I did."

"Damn. That's some kinda… I dunno. That's so cool of him. Really." Her smile grew. "Um, what kinda art do you do?"

"I paint."

"You any good? I mean, I guess you have to sorta be since you got a scholarship and all, but really what—"

"I get by."

"I'd like to see your work sometime. I mean…if you want me to…"

She stepped down onto the sidewalk, smiling, her defenses melting. "We'll see. Right now we've got a date with some chili." Down the street she ran, giggling now. Pouring on the speed. Something nice to follow, better inspiration than saving his stupid brother's life.

Out of breath, Wendell caught up. "So this…*pant*…is our second date?"

"Do you *ever* give up?"

"Not when there's…*puff*…a worthy prize at the finish line."

Running alongside her, Wendell saw a bit of red touch her cheeks, blushing. Or mortified, hard to say with her. A quick change in attitude, she pulled ahead, and said, "Time's running out."

For a moment, Wendell'd forgotten his looming deadline. "Crap…what time is it?"

Like magic, her phone materialized in her hand (and where in hell did she keep it anyway?). "Eleven-oh-three. That gives us what, twenty-nine minutes?"

"Yeah. Dammit. I mean if I push it, *really* push it, I can run an eight-minute mile. We—"

"That's all?" Ahead of him, she ran backward, showing off a little. "I can do seven-and-a-half, maybe less. No sweat."

Wendell believed it, too. She hadn't broken a sweat yet. Glistened with beauty a little, but definitely no perspiration. Still, a competitor at heart, Wendell wouldn't concede. "No way! Prove it!"

"You're on." She turned around, and tore off at a sprinter's pace. Wendell followed, trying to cover his labored breathing.

"About half…a mile…to go," he panted out. "Little over…two miles back. We might…just make it…barely."

"Then we'll have to go faster."

They hammered through the intersection at McGee, traffic dwindling to a rare trickle. In this neck of the woods, most of Kansas City had retreated for the night. Except for the bad element, of course, the folks Wendell'd become quite acquainted with in the last several hours.

Next to them sat an abandoned parking lot, weeds growing through the cracked pavement, life striving to survive on a derelict landscape. Moonlight painted Alicia's face a sickly blue color, unsettling in a way. Wendell shivered, hoped her corpse-like pallor wasn't forewarning of things to come.

They pounded across the pavement, their shadows stretching as if trying to outrun the owners.

"So…why'd you assume I was a Republican anyway?" he asked in an attempt to keep his mind occupied.

"You're going there again? Really?"

"Hey, you pretty much raked my flaws over the coals. Surely you got a couple that needs raking. Maybe."

"Just because I'm almost perfect, doesn't mean I am." Had she not been smiling, had Wendell not come to understand her better, he might've written her off again for being stuck up as he had the first time. But, he thought, shared trauma kicks down doors. "I guess I shouldn't have made that assumption. Pretty dumb of me."

"You think?"

"Usually. But there was your back story, Midwest kid from a family of bankers. And…I've been out with guys like you before. All talk, all swagger, all bluster. Always Republicans."

"Hellooo! Assumptions again! 'Guys like me.' Tshhh, right. They broke the mold when they made me!"

"Maybe they just scraped the mold off you."

"Funny."

"I think so. Anyway, lesson learned. No more assumptions."

"About time." An extremely mild bit of payback, but it tasted sweet nonetheless. "To tell you the truth, though… You'd never know it, but I used to be Republican. Back when I didn't know any better, the way my parents pretty much browbeat it into—"

"Yeah, yeah, yeah. You rebelled. The record's stuck, Wendell."

"Crap. I told you all that, too?"

"Yep. Damn open book you were. I couldn't wait to shut it."

"Is there anything I didn't tell you that night? My underwear size, maybe?"

She glanced down, an eyebrow tantalizingly up. "No. But, it's kinda a moot point now."

"Oh, yeah. Right."

They sidled out of the parking lot, back to the sidewalk. Alicia slowed, stuck an arm out in front of Wendell, forcing a halt.

"What's wrong?" As soon as he asked it, he knew. Ahead, at the corner of Oak and 11th, the Jackson County City Hall towered, the cement hand of local justice. Patrol cars lined the street. Two cops strolled up the steps. One stood outside smoking, taking his time.

"Dammit!" Wendell grabbed Alicia's arm, and steered her into the shadows of the building behind them. "Obviously, we can't run past them. Other options?"

"Across the street's the Illus Davis Civic Park. It's, like, two blocks long. But…we might run into some patrolling cops. Or worse."

"*Worse*? How in hell could this night get any worse?"

"Wanna find out?" This time Wendell saw something reckless in her eyes, a daredevil side he hadn't seen before. Maybe he'd better cap her adrenaline before it overflowed and drowned them.

"Alicia, look, I appreciate everything you've done for me. But you don't have to go any farther. Things might go south. Fast, you know? Go home, be safe. I can do this on—Ow!"

"You think *that* hurt?"

How do you answer that question? "Um…no?" Wendell massaged his arm where she'd hit him.

"I'll kick your ass if you think you're gonna pat me on the head, call me a good little girl, and send me home. Waving your sexist flag again! We're in it together!"

He liked the sound of "together" quite a bit. Just not the rest of it. "Again…*not* sexist."

"So you keep sayin'! Maybe—"

Grmble…rumble, rummm…

"Crap! The boys are back in town!"

Southbound on Oak, the Impala charged toward them, tires screaming. A hell of a time for the smoking cop to vanish into the city hall.

On instinct—inherent sexism?—Wendell grabbed Alicia's hand, tugged her along behind him. She wriggled free from his grip, and easily paced him. Across 10th Street, the park sprawled across a couple of blocks. Lamp sentinels stood tall and proud through the grounds, erasing crucial shadows. But they couldn't just sit where they were.

The car sped toward them, dangerously fast. Headlights chocked into bright. Wendell and Alicia dashed across the street, strides wide, practically leaping for the relative safety of the park.

"I see your ass, Wendy!" Little Ben screamed.

Not wanting to meet the lash of Jiggy's whip, not to mention 4,000 pounds of rushing metal, Wendell gave it his all. Alicia ran even faster and surged ahead. A good thing. Maybe Ben's crew wouldn't realize they were together.

Alicia bounded onto the sidewalk and into the park. Wendell followed, his gaze focused on her top-knot bobbing back and forth. Next to the park, the Impala's brakes locked up.

"Get him, Jiggy!" ordered Little Ben.

A car door opened, and slammed shut. Footsteps clocked through the street. The car zipped ahead, down Oak and turned onto 11th Street. Fortunately, 11th Street ran one way, the opposite direction of the park. Buying them a little more time.

Jiggy entered the park. Sharp firecracker pops accompanied his pursuit.

For a park, concrete islands and stairs comprised the natural order of things, nature practically extinct. Flagpoles and lampposts outnumbered trees. Wendell and Alicia could tear it up across the pavement, but it left nowhere to hide.

Like rats in a maze, they wound around raised cement islands, the turns unending, unable to kick into a straight, speedy trajectory.

Wendell glanced back. Jiggy narrowed the distance between them, coming on strong. His love for his whip, though, slowed him down. He grunted, cursed. On a backswing, the whip lash wrapped around his legs. He tumbled to the ground.

"Now's our chance," said Wendell. More than a leap of faith, they took three steps at a time, ran a short spurt, then descended more steps pointlessly going nowhere. Ahead lay a large man-made pool of water, the moon's light rippling off the surface.

"Around the reflecting pool," said Alicia.

Aptly titled, the pool perfectly reflected Wendell's fear. In the moon-dappled water, he glimpsed his pale, frightened face, his even paler body.

The whip cracked again. On his feet again, Jiggy plodded along behind them, slower as if losing interest or victim of a two-pack-a-day habit.

The pool—and what a very stupid place to drop a pool, Wendell thought—finally ended. They rounded the perimeter and bounded up six wide steps. A statue loomed over them—undoubtedly the park's titular Ilus Davis—cocksure in his relaxed stance and wonderful suit that Wendell'd kill to be wearing.

"Gonna *get* you," called out Jiggy, sounding distant, a world away. The constant slap of the whip slowed to infrequent pops.

Across the park, a flashlight's beam swept their way. "Hey! Stop!"

"Dammit," said Alicia, "the cops. Come on!"

Up the stairs they flew, two at a time, to Locust Street. Completely bereft of street lamps, Locust provided lots of shadows to fade into.

"As I walk through the valley of the shadow of death…"

The tell-tale music of Ben's crew thumped along to the beat of Wendell's heart. Slowly growing louder. Apparently following the speed limit for a change due to the proximity of City Hall.

The cop in the park called out something again, his flashlight bouncing as he ran. His radio crackled, followed by more shouts, each one more distraught than the last. Wendell would've loved to introduce the cop to Little Ben and the boys. On the bright side, Jiggy had gone silent.

The Impala ambled down Locust, motor growling like a dog ready to bite. Wendell and Alicia cut across Locust at an angle. Around the corner, they entered 10th Street, the worst neighborhood Wendell'd literally run across yet. From dark alleyways and abandoned buildings, Wendell felt eyes watching them.

Back on Locust, the music mounted steadily. Coming for them.

"They been spending most their lives living in a gangstas paradise…"

Wendell ducked into an alley, dragging Alicia after him. "I mean it," he said, "you *have* to go. We need to separate. If we split up, they'll follow me. Maybe they haven't even seen you yet."

"Doubtful since we were linked at the wrist when we crossed the street."

Good point. Bad outlook.

The music thumped, a jarring, jangling soundtrack playing to Wendell's nerves. The Impala's motor revved up again.

Wendell scanned the neighborhood, hoping for a Hail, Mary. He found one in the form of a utilitarian, gray-bricked building set back a good distance from the street. With a flat slate roof and a single long window, it resembled a poor man's prison. Gravel filled the parking lot. So did trucks, lots of pickup trucks. Honestly, it didn't appear too inviting, but fingers of light reached from behind drawn curtains. The simple sign out front, a cheap one with removable plastic letters, shone like a beacon of hope: *Brotherhood Hall – Meeting tonite.*

"There! I'll be all right there until the crew passes." Wendell pointed toward the building catty-corner from them. "You go up 10th, circle back. And run for your life, Alicia! Don't stop."

"You kidding me? Wendell, you don't know *who's* in that building. They might be—"

"'Brotherhood Hall', Alicia! Duh! Boy Scouts, V.A. guys, I don't care, Shriners, they're proclaimed brothers! They're not gonna turn a guy down in a time of need."

They couldn't see the Impala. But they heard it, motor humming but traveling nowhere. Maybe the park cop had stopped them. Or possibly they were waiting for Jiggy to rejoin the fun, plotting some kind of new torture.

Maybe Wendell and Alicia needed to get the hell

out of there, argue later.

"Give me the bracelet, Alicia." Wendell held his hand out, and wouldn't move until she relinquished the parcel.

She clutched it to her chest, a prized possession. "I'm going with you."

"Give it to me!" He reached for it. She whirled, her back toward Wendell. "Just shut up and let's go!"

"For God's—" Before Wendell could stop her, she zipped by him. Out in the street, a perfect target for Ben's guys.

The Impala erupted. Tires burned. On the move again.

Alicia crossed 10th, darted into an empty corner lot overgrown with weeds. Wendell followed her into the field, the scraggly weeds itching his calves. Running at full force, chasing Alicia.

Headlights roamed over their backs, flit over the field, swung back into the street as the Impala straightened onto 10th.

"Where ya goin' now, Wendy?" cried Little Ben. "Goddammit! Hit the brakes!"

The car stopped, hell on wheels.

"Alicia, don't…do…this!" Nearly caught up to her, Wendell reached out, tried to grab her arm. Realized how stupid that was as he'd send them both crashing down. Nothing could stop her now anyway. Part of why he liked her, he realized, for better or for worse as the wedding vows go.

Alicia ran smack into the building. She yanked on the left handle of the red double doors. Locked. A domino effect, Wendell practically slammed into her. A quick look back. The Impala sat in the street opposite the field, engine revving. Waiting for Wendell’s next move.

Wendell started to wonder just how badly Big Ben wanted his stupid chili, probably something he should’ve considered earlier.

Regardless, if Ben’s crew hadn’t seen Alicia before, they had now. Not that Wendell seemed to have a say in the matter, but she was most definitely, irrefutably all in now. In over her head and drowning right next to Wendell.

He didn’t know whether to hug or chew her out. Both would have to wait. Hands cupped around his eyes, he peered through the tiny door window, no bigger than a porthole. Welcome, warm light illuminated the interior lobby. “At least stay in the lobby while I check the building out first. You keep an eye on the fun boys. Let me know if they make a move, ’kay?”

Not agreeing nor disagreeing, friggin’ Sweden, she said nothing, pulled at the right door’s handle. It opened. Wendell sidled in front of her. As soon as she slipped in behind him, he pulled the door shut. A chain clanked. No lock, nothing, just a useless metal chain wrapped around the push handle.

“Look, I need you to stay here, okay?”

She half-smirked, looked doubtful, and ended up shaking her head in a resigned fashion. On tiptoes, she peered out the window.

Wendell heard voices beyond the next set of doors—good-natured, laughing, exactly what he’d expect from a brotherhood, his faith in humanity restored. He set his face in sad-sack, woeful mode, tried to ignore his lack of clothing, and opcncd thc door.

At the far end of what looked like a theatre, a group of men sat in a circle in front of a stage. Meager ceiling lights touched the men's bowed heads, apparently lost in prayer. Wendell cleared his throat. Heads raised, swiveled toward him. Folding chairs creaked. Silence followed, a lack of sound Wendell'd come to dread tonight.

One man stood, notepad in hand waving about extravagantly. "Welcome, brother, welcome!"

"Ah…hi." Bit by wary bit, Wendell approached the gathered men. On his left and right, rows of folding chairs lined up perfectly, their white backs like tombstones at Arlington Cemetery.

Mumbles, grumbles and salutations warmed up to Wendell. "Hello…looks like you've had a bad night," said one of them. "Believe me, brother, you've found the right place."

Relieved, Wendell said, "Man, I hope so. You wouldn't *believe* the night I've had! My name's Wendell and I—"

In chorus, "Welcome, Wendell."

Wendell stopped short, felt damn short as more of the men stood. Some of them applauded, smiles all around. It hit him he'd stumbled into an AA meeting or some kind of variation. No matter. He'd gladly become an alcoholic for a night if they'd loan him pants or offer protection. Shameless, of course. Wendell added it to the list of his other crimes tonight. There'd be a whole lot of charity work in his future to atone for his trespasses.

"Thanks, guys, but I need a favor. I'm in…" As he moved closer toward them, the applause stopped. Smiles dropped like calls from his crappy cell phone.

Best not to rock their already hole-filled boats. "Yeah, anyway, I, uh…I'm…" Wendell hitchhiked a thumb behind him. His words drifted away, his train of logic derailed. Things seemed off in a night ripe with off.

All white guys. Most of them sporting shaved heads. Not a real problem, kinda weird in this neighborhood, though. And a lot of them showing ink on their heads, their necks, their…

Uh-oh.

Two flags flanked the stage. One, the Confederate flag. The other, the Nazi flag.

Ohhh, it's that *kind of "brotherhood."*

He couldn't come up with a better escape plan, so he went with the first thing that popped into his head: "Hey, guys, I left my phone in my pants, so…" He turned, bumping into Alicia.

Wendell shrieked. Alicia shrieked, too.

"They're coming," she said. "They're in the field now."

All of this proved upsetting. But the group behind Wendell concerned him first and foremost.

"Hey! She a China girl?" shouted the leader.

"*What*?" screamed Alicia. "What the hell is this, Wendell? A KKK rally?" She shoved Wendell aside to address the racists in the room. "You callin' me a China girl, pig?"

Scratch Wendell's previous thought: Alicia's response by far proved most upsetting.

He leaned over, and whispered, "We have to go. *Now*." Their odds seemed better against three gangstas rather than a mob of Aryans.

Too little, too late. Hurricane Alicia had been unleashed. "I'm *not* gonna put up with this crap! You guys are a buncha—"

"Wendell, we thought you was one a' us. You takin' up with a chink?" The men looked serious, scary serious. Coming their way now, hands fisted, growling.

"Yeah, what's the matter, Wendell? Our kind not good enough fer ya?" This guy, the biggest of the bunch, moved like a cat, quiet and altogether terrifying.

"Sorry we intruded, guys, meant nothin' by it. We'll just be going now." Hands up, pleading mercy. Wendell backed away, shielding Alicia—more like trying to keep her at bay—and pushing her toward the doors.

Alicia struggled to get around Wendell, ready to go twelve rounds. Wonder Woman and her bullet-deflecting wristbands. "Don't you *dare* apologize to these asshats, Wendell! They—"

"Huh. You know, Wendell," said the leader, "I thought your name sounded a little Jewie. Chinks and Hebes rootin' together. Whaddaya think about that, boys?"

"Get 'em!"

With some experience in dealing with enraged mobs under his belt, Wendell knew better than to try to spin a golden weave of words. He grabbed Alicia's wrist. Yanked her out of her warrior's stance and hauled her behind him. A stream of expletives flew from her mouth, really stirring it up.

Chairs thwacked down as more of the men rose. Someone kicked a chair, primed no doubt from many years of Donahue viewing. Someone sailed a chair over their heads. A dozen racists ran for them.

"Jesus!" yelled Wendell.

"Don't you *dare* say his name, Jew-boy!"

Cries of war rose. Flames of hatred nearly torched the brotherhood hall.

Wendell raced for the door, Alicia in tow. His hand sweaty, Wendell gripped the door handle. Slipped. Tried again. It flew open the same time the outer door cracked back.

Little Ben and Bodacious froze, guns in hand. Eyes wide. Mouths forming little "Oh, hells."

Jiggy burst between them, the whip held above him. He spoke before looking, never a wise practice. "Where is he? Where's Wendy? I'm gonna…"

"Hah!" Wendell couldn't help it. Nearly hysterical, he followed with "Booyah!"

Quieter than church. Wendell looked behind him. The Aryan mob swiveled their heads—slow, dumb like a cow's tail—back and forth between Wendell, Alicia, and the newcomers. The tide turned, ready to go Tsunami on Little Ben. Wendell and Alicia were all but forgotten.

"That darkie got a *whip*? Jumpin' Jesus, boy, you lookin' for payback from slavin' days? Gonna take it out on us, your betters?"

"Let's make sure they know their places!"

"Get 'em!"

To get out of the line of fire, Wendell tugged Alicia aside. Draped his arms around her, hugged her close, then hugged the wall. Anchored in solidly and waiting for the storm to pass. Plus it kinda felt nice.

Screams blistered into death threats. One of the Nazis whistled Dixie. Roars and hollers. Like an ill-wind, hate violence blew through the hall until they took it outside.

And Wendell kept hugging. No struggle, no

dissent, Alicia the calm in his storm. Wendell looked into her eyes, her endless depths of eyes. Her gaze flitted down to his lips, back toward his eyes. Her lips parted, just a hair, wanting. Wendell leaned in with closed eyes and kissed her fingers.

Mission aborted!

She pressed her finger of steel against Wendell's lips, this time more forceful than before. She kept pushing until their embrace broke.

"We gotta go." Simple, direct, to the point. No flirting, no desire, nothing. A robot. How could Wendell have misread her so badly?

Or maybe he was *still* the reigning king of bad timing.

Yeah, he told himself, *that's what it is. She wants to kiss, but now's not the time*.

Rallying after a minor setback, Wendell clapped his hands, gave a sorta half-hearted hop, said, "Okay, let's finish this!"

Cautiously, they opened the doors. They strolled out casually as if exiting church. Out on 10th Street, Little Ben's men had miraculously made it to their car. The Aryans surrounded it, one guy standing on the hood. The others rocked the car, the engine sputtering to come to life. Someone, Bodacious probably, laid down on the horn. A bullet fired through a crack in the window. Which just made the skinheads angrier. A new round of battle cries erupted. Just a good ol' time in Dixie.

"Serves them right," said Wendell, watching the event, fascinated, front row at a boxing match.

"I dunno. Kinda wish Little Ben would cap a few of their asses. Make it hard for them to sit for a while."

"You're *sooo* gangsta," said Wendell. "Anyway, that'll tie them up for a while. Let's get outta here before more bullets start flying."

"Wait." She bridged a hand megaphone around her mouth. "Nazi, stupid, racist, narrow-minded *asshats*!"

"Dammit! Death wish much?" Wendell pulled her away before she'd unleash more of her wrath.

"Ah, they didn't hear me," she said. "I guess a black guy with a whip trumps me." Her shoulders slumped, almost disappointed. Endearing in an unusual way.

"Let's just get outta here. Go get chili. Save my stupid brother. Get clothes. In that order." Natch, he left out how he envisioned the grand finale: a loving kiss from his partner, a pledge to lifetime happiness. Cue the swelling violins, all eyes in the theatre misty.

Jesus, I really do need to live life more.

"Which way now?" asked Wendell.

Always one step ahead of him, she'd already taken off. "Goin' as far as we can down 10th, then gradually work back to 12th. You waiting for a bus or something?"

And, man, did that ever sound like a good idea. Wendell's feet hurt, possibly to the point of swelling. Thigh muscles he didn't know he had screamed for mercy. His lower legs and calves pounded like migraines gone south. Tired, weary, sweaty, naked, miserable, scratched, and itchy.

And completely, ludicrously head over heels in love.

He ran and kept running, Alicia beside him.

Wendell had something to prove: to his brother, to Alicia, especially to himself. Time to shine. Time to live life. Make a difference. Be a hero.

A second (Third? Fourth?) wind puffed his sails out. He dialed up the speed, smoked by Alicia. A challenge for her to run faster. Both of them grinned as they raced toward their chili date.

They turned onto Cherry street, sprinting down to 11th. City lights were rare in this area, everyone in their right mind tucked in bed. Almost pleasant, no one else around but them. Their footfalls echoed off of the cement and brick guardians of the night.

"Down to 12th Street?" she asked.

"Let's do it."

On the opposite side of Cherry lay a block-long parking lot. They took advantage, made up crucial seconds, cut through the corner lot to 12th.

Back on track and in the home stretch.

"Not too much farther." Alicia huffed it out between breaths, her first sign of fatigue.

Wendell's heart beat hard. His lungs expelled shallow and quick bursts of air. "So…back there, didn't you maybe realize that pissing off a roomful of neo-Nazis probably isn't the best thing for a long and healthy life?"

Hard to do while running, but she managed a shrug anyway. "That stuff just really gets to me, you know?"

"Yeah."

"No, you don't. Not really. I mean, you're white, privileged."

Good grief! One step forward, two jumps back.

"Not this routine again, Alicia."

"There's nothing routine about me, dammit!" She stopped. But they had no time for it, not now. Wendell circled around her. Trying to get her back in the game.

"That's probably true," he said. "But let's finish this. We'll talk later, 'kay?"

"All right." Her lips pinched together in a painful looking way. She set out, her anger apparently focused on the run.

Yet he was the one who went there again. Couldn't be helped. "You want me to apologize for being white? I'm sorry. It's not my fault. And I'm not exactly what you'd call privileged either."

"There's a difference. You chose not to be."

"I did. Because it's not who I am. And…I guess I don't know about racism. Not really. But…all through school I was picked on. Bullied."

"You? Why?"

Here it came, the one bombshell he was sure he didn't blurt out on his disastrous, drunken date. The secret he'd wanted to take with him to the grave and beyond. "Cause I was overweight."

Her feet stuttered, tripped up a bit, before she gathered speed again. "You? You were fat? I mean…really you're kinda scrawny."

"Hey, thanks for the kind words! And I prefer 'pleasantly plump.' That's what my mom used to call me."

"Jeeze…"

"Ah, it is what it is. Anyway, I learned to run from bullies. Found out it was also a good way to drop weight. Anyway, if you ever felt ostracized…because you were different, *are* different…I felt the same way."

"Not *really* the same, because—"

"Oh, of course! Your pain was *much* worse than mine."

"*Now* who's assuming crap, Wendell? You're

impossible!"

"And you're not?"

"Look, your bullying was based on something you could do something about. You could change! And you did! I'll always be Asian."

"Don't those shoulder chips weigh you down? You carry 'em around like, I dunno, shoulder pads from the eighties or somethin'!"

He took aim, released his trigger finger. Apparently he hit her bullseye. She said nothing in return. Quietly she ran, pondering her feet. Completely unlike her. Usually she held her shoulders up, her gaze high, the tallest person in Kansas City.

"Sorry," said Wendell, "I didn't mean to hurt—"

"No, you're right. I kinda do look for fights sometimes. Even when there really aren't any to be had."

As always, Wendell had a lot to say, but for once, decided to let her run with it. Her trip, after all.

"I grew up in a multi-cultural neighborhood. Even there, racism was everywhere, between people you wouldn't expect it to be. Worse, my folks insisted on sending me to a suburban school in a white neighborhood. I don't know how they swung that, but…that's neither here nor there. I guess I went in expecting to be treated differently. And I was. Just not the way I thought I'd be. I became…sort of a pet project, a lab experiment to the rich girls. They didn't like me for who I was. They liked me for *what* I was. And when they'd had enough of their 'multi-cultural' experience, they'd dump me. It happened every year. I got used to it. And swore I wouldn't go through it ever again."

"You know…I'm not all about that, right?" It slowed him down, running in a sort of sideways shuffle next to her. But a talk like this demanded attention.

"I think I do now, Wendell." She smiled, then swiped a strand of magenta hair behind her ear. "We gonna have a cry-fest now or what?"

"I'd rather have a chili-fest."

As they ran across Holmes, commercial buildings vanished, replaced by vacant lots and grave, brick-faced, low-income housing. Toys scattered the yards and Wendell wondered why no one bothered stealing them. Maybe the kids packed heat here. Everyone else in the Midwest seemed to own a gun.

The landscape changed. Almost early Western prairie compared to the always-on-the-move civilization of downtown proper. Yet signs of gentrification drifted in, too, as sure as the tide. *Coming Soon* signs and landscaping heralded the changing of a neighborhood, not necessarily for the better. It puzzled Wendell where the low-income people kept migrating to, chased out of downtown already to make room for those who could afford the renovated dwellings.

They crossed beneath Highway 70. The sudden reemergence of civilization roaring above Wendell's head startled him, waking him from the peculiar surreal dreaminess of the isolated last tour of their run. Surrounded by the underpass' stone walls, Wendell clamped his hands over his ears at the deafening sound until they exited the other side.

Alicia laughed, and said, "You can come up for air now."

He dropped his hands, forcing a grin. "Tender ears."

"More like tender foot." This time she dropped the challenge and raced ahead. Maybe just doing it to goad him to the finish line.

They pushed on across Troost, past Paseo, entering the most fabled and crime-ridden parts of Kansas City. Boarded-up houses became the norm, the bulk of the neighborhood. Several times he thought he saw lights—nothing more than a matches' worth—blinking between gaps in the boards.

"It's so quiet," said Wendell.

"What'd you expect? Constant gunfire? Screams in the night? Sirens 24-7? War-torn Kansas City?"

Kinda. "No, don't be ridiculous."

Two blocks of absolute darkness threatened to swallow them as they ran into it. Alicia's mystery phone reappeared, serving as a lamp to guide them. It reminded Wendell of a Sherlock Holmes flick where a character carried a lantern across the foggy moors.

To keep frightening thoughts at bay, Wendell resumed their conversation. Barely above a whisper, though. No sense in stirring the dead. "So…earlier you said my book sounds boring."

"Yep." Snapped that one right out there, no pause for "maybe" or "I'd have to read it" or "I didn't *really* mean it."

"I've been thinking."

"Uh oh."

"Maybe it is. The book, I mean. Boring."

He laughed, hollow as he felt. Here in his underwear, on the streets of K.C., his book did seem a little underwhelming. Maybe it was time to give up pursuit of his own Moby Dick. Then he realized how lousy that metaphor turned out. "*What* was I thinking?

A Pocketful of Heart. Damn. I may as well've called it *A Lungful of Love*. Or…or…how about *A Bowel Movement of Bravery*?"

For the first time that night, she really cut loose. Her laughter rose above them, shrill, yet melodic. "Stop! I can't run if I'm laughing! Wait! I got it! *An Intestine of Integrity*!"

"Hah! Good one!"

"Wait, Wendell…here comes inspiration!" Playfully, she swooned, the back of her hand against her forehead as if channeling Shirley MacLaine. "*Nostrils of Naiveté*! No! *A Bra full of Brazenness*! Even better! *A Jock-Strap of—*"

"Okay, okay… I think we're done now." Glad for the darkness, Wendell flared red, deeply embarrassed. A mighty big difference between good-humored self-mockery and kicking a writer while he's down.

After Alicia wound down her giggle fit, she said, "Wendell?"

"Hmm?"

"You know when I said no one wants to read your *Pocketful* book?"

"Kinda hard to forget something like that."

"Don't quit writing."

"What?"

She tapped him on the shoulder, smiling. "Keep writing. I have no doubt you're gonna be great."

"Really? But you said *A Pocketful of—*"

"Boring. I know, right? Sorry if it hurt you. But I never suggested you should stop writing. It's your dream, right?"

"Yeah, I guess so."

"There's that overwhelming confidence. Follow

your dream."

"But…what do I write about? I mean that book's been, like, building in my head since I was a kid and—"

Alicia put her brakes on again, wheeled on him. Wendell had to dance into a side-step to avoid colliding. "*Listen* to yourself! Quit obsessing! Start over! This time with something you've lived through, something that means something. Something—"

"Like *what*?"

Hands on hips, she gave him that disgusted look, the one he'd grown accustomed to and—God help him—somewhat fond of. "Oh, my *Gawd… Seriously*? If I have to tell you, maybe you're *not* a writer!"

She waited for enlightenment to strike, for the clock to clang, for light bulbs to flash brilliantly above Wendell's head.

Nothing. Crickets. Nobody home. Lights out at the Worthy estate of mind.

When she flicked a finger against his temple, a couple of lights—more like an electric jolt— flipped on.

He threw his arms up above him. Field goal! *Duh.*

"You're right! I've been threatened by vicious drug dealers, chased by the homeless, held at shotgun by a priest, belittled by a bachelorette party and a particularly nasty doorman…" She frowned. "…forced to striptease in front of a bevy of gay bears (are bears in a bevy? Always wondered that), nearly whipped in my underwear, pursued by a parole officer, interrupted a skinhead AA meeting (and wouldn't you kinda think alcoholism is just sorta one of their requirements?) and all the time had my trusty sidekick—"

"*Not* a sidekick."

"Okay, my potential love interest at my side."

"Better."

"All in the name of chili to save my loud-mouth, dumb-ass brother and did you say 'better' just now when I called you my potential love interest?"

"Actions speak better than words." On tiptoes, she reached up, grabbed Wendell by the ears, levered him down. And kissed him.

Short and more than sweet.

She released him, sort of tossed his head back. Her phone angled sideways, the light dancing mischievously in her eyes.

"Is this the happily ever after?" asked Wendell, still stunned, still sky-high. Hell, he felt airless, ready to skywrite with his fingertips: *Wendell hearts Alicia.*

"How about a 'to be continued'," she said. "Let's finish this. Just over the hill, one and a half blocks or so to *Marion's Eats and Drinks*."

"Let's do it!" *Let's* again. Such a wonderful word. One that kickstarted his tighty-whities—now owning them, dammit—back into running.

They chugged up a hill, descended, raced beneath a small bridge. Lights filled the intersection ahead. Not a mirage, but the real thing after a long haul through the desert.

Two small strip malls sat across from one another, mostly comprised of brick and flat roofs, basically chimneys. Poor signage hung out front, pleading for customer attention. Small eateries, a convenience store barred up like a jail cell, a hairdresser, and competing fingernail salons sat across from each other. And just beyond that: *Marion's Eats and Drinks*!

The sign in the yard—nothing more than a

glorified church sign announcing a weekly special of ribs instead of sermon content—had several bulbs out, rendering it nearly unreadable.

At long last, the finish line. The building set off the road, half hidden by the strip mall next to it. Wendell approached the sign, felt a benchmark moment—one he'd memorialize in his first true book—tapped it like a trusty dog.

Together, Wendell and Alicia trudged toward the steepled building, pitched somewhere between a red brick oven and a barn. Sparse lighting fell out from the front window and stretched across the lawn.

Wendell had to be first, the proper way to end this. He'd earned it. He bypassed Alicia.

"Wendell, wait," called Alicia. "I'd better be the one to go in. You know…your tighty-whities?"

He didn't hear her. Maybe he did, but it didn't matter. His legs had numbed to the point of nearly going asleep, muscles maxed out. He plodded toward the door, moving awkwardly, stomping toward Marion's like a toddler taking his first steps. He felt a little dread, some exhilaration, mostly exhaustion. A moment to savor, he couldn't believe the end had finally come, just like Christmas morning.

He gripped the doorknob. Pulled. Expected refreshing air conditioning to wash over him. Instead, he met with resistance. Locked.

Oh, goddammit, no, it can't be locked!

Wendell tried the knob again, surely it'd just slipped in his sweaty palm. Same outcome. He yanked at the doors. Rattled them. Leaned back, plopped his feet up onto the door and pulled until his butt slid down to the ground. With his feet and hands still planted on the glass, he rode the door into delirium.

Oblivious to everything but Fate's cruel joke, Wendell didn't feel Alicia's hand on his shoulder, not really.

"Um, Wendell?" She drew his attention toward a cheap cardboard sign, damn happy lettering scrawled across it: *Closed*! In smaller letters beneath it: *Sorry! Come again between 10:00 A.M. to 11:00 P.M.*

Wendell hated the sign, imagined it teasing him with a snarky voice close to Vincent the doorman's.

"*Noooo!* No, no, no! You *can't* be closed, dammit! After everything I've *been* through tonight!"

"Wendell? It's eleven-fourteen. We missed it by fourteen minutes."

"*Nooooo*!" Still the only person in the world, Wendell didn't see the janitor, not at first.

The janitor—Marion himself, maybe?—wore an apron and a huge, surly frown. He waddled over, carrying his broom like a weapon he wasn't afraid to use. He stared down at Wendell, disgusted. *Peeved*, for God's sake! He shook his head, tapped the *Closed* sign. Enunciated his words carefully and loudly. "*Closed*. You read English? Closed, cryin' out loud, closed! Come back tomorrow! Bring pants!"

"You don't understand!" Still pulling at the door like it'd magically open, Wendell raised his voice, ready to raise the roof if it gained him entrance. "My brother's gonna *die* if I don't get some of your *stupid* chili! *Please*, mister, it's a life-or-death emergency! You *gotta*—"

"Sorry, come back tomorrow! Sleep it off! Go home! Tomorrow I fix you up good!"

"*Open* these damn doors! Open 'em now, dammit!

I stripped in front of a buncha' bears for your *chiliii*!"

"Wendell, stop it. There's nothing we can do. I'm sorry…"

"You don't leave me alone," said the janitor, "I'll call the cops! Go *home*!" He dismissed Wendell with an "ah, crazy" hand gesture. With a shuffling limp, he disappeared into the back.

Still working the doors, Wendell growled at their uncooperative state. He jumped up. Felt wild, out of control, ready for anything. Because he'd already been through everything else. Like a wildman, he dug fingers into his hair, raised it like a clown's perf.

"Jesus, Wendell, you tried. That's it. It's time to go to the cops and—"

"And nothing! Wait! I got an idea! Shoulda' thought of it earlier."

He brushed by Alicia, her presence barely registering on Wendell's zoned-out radar.

From far away: "Wendell, wait! What're you *doing?* You're acting psycho-nuts! Stop it!"

In the street-side rock garden, he foraged. Pushed rocks over until he found a worthy one. Amped adrenaline hulked his strength. He hefted the huge rock over his head, didn't feel any strain.

"Dammit, Wendell, put the rock down!" Alicia, frustrated, held her phone out, no doubt primed to dial 911. "What're you going to—"

"I'm gonna throw this rock through the glass window, jump in, get some chili, that's what I'm gonna do. Oh, would you leave a few bucks for a tip?"

Crazy, out of his mind, he knew it and didn't give a damn. He staggered toward the glass window, boulder above his head, growing lighter by the minute. Both the boulder and his head…

Chapter Eight

11:10 P.M.

Frustrated and famished, Dayton Bookes cruised by the Brotherhood Hall, home of downtown K.C.'s finest, upstanding neo-nazis, not to mention the latest sighting of Landers' ankle monitor. What he saw astounded him. Rather, tickled might be more accurate and Dayton didn't tickle easy. Only if you hit his special spot just right, the one beneath his ribs, to the side…

Dayton considered stopping, maybe right some injustices, but frankly, all he saw were injustices battling it out. Definitely Benjamin Landers' car, a tricked-out Impala, under siege by a gang of skinheads. Let the worst man win, survival of the inept. Besides, Dayton was sorely outnumbered and ill-equipped to go into such a situation. And he had a job to do. Plenty of cops just a couple blocks away. He'd phone it in. More than either side of the combatants deserved.

"…and, Sergeant?"

"Yeah, Bookes?"

"Pretty damn sure at least some of 'em are packin'. Be careful breaking up their little party. Stick 'em in the same holding cell if you're feelin' particularly fun-loving."

The Sergeant chuckled. "See what we can

accommodate at our luxury hotel. Any idea what the hell's goin' on?"

"Something hinky. And I aim to iron out the hinks."

Whatever was happening, Dayton knew Landers was up to his shiny, golden teeth in it. Somehow the Strawberry was key. Odd company the kid had been keeping tonight. First Landers and crew, then the homeless, next the gays, and finally the white supremacist jackasses. To Dayton, the kid looked like he'd be more at home sipping latte in a coffee house. What did all of the Strawberry's pals have in common? From what Dayton'd just seen, none of them would be singing Kumbaya together anytime soon.

His phone beeped. The green blip on the move again. Making serious time, especially if on foot, passing Troost, Paseo, and keepin' on. Dayton'd grown so used to calling the mystery kid a "Strawberry," he almost wished the green blip was a little red strawberry or something, like PacMan.

Dayton turned right, blasted through an empty intersection, and hung a left on 12th.

Where the hell is he going? Not a good 'hood for Strawberries.

The phone blurted again. Don't text and drive, he knew the rule, but still, he had to look. The Strawberry had landed, somewhere around 12th and Brooklyn. Didn't appear to be leaving either.

With the end of the pursuit in mind, Dayton stepped on the gas pedal.

Hang tight, Strawberry, Bookes is coming to find out what makes you run.

The intersection ahead of his destination, Dayton

slowed the Taurus, looked left and right, never one to fully trust the GPS. On the left, a sign: *Marion's Eats and Drinks*.

And, damn! Sure enough, target spotted. The kid, near naked in his tighty-whities, stood in front of Marion's ready to hurl a big rock through the window.

Dayton wheeled the Taurus into Marion's drive-thru lane. Popped over the curb, and hammered the brakes. The car fishtailed in the rock garden. Small pebbles flung up and landed on the hood like a hail storm. His headlights lit up the Strawberry in all his glory. He switched them to bright, gave the kid a little nudie spotlight. Kid didn't seem to notice. Gun in hand, Dayton scrambled out of the car. His jacket caught on the car door, snagged his arm back. The gun clacked to the pavement.

"Freeze, Strawberry, police!" Even though his gun sat at his feet, he pulled out all authoritarian vocal tricks.

Strawberry froze, didn't turn. He didn't drop the rock either. Next to him, a girl had her hands out, pleading to the Strawberry by the looks of things.

Dayton pulled an uncomfortable deep knee bend, and snatched his gun. "Dammit, drop the rock! To the ground, I mean!"

"*Wendell!*" the girl screamed, now wringing out panic. "He's got a *gun*! Do as he *says*!"

The Strawberry eeked out something, no louder than a mouse on a brave day. Still held that rock above his head like some Greek God ready to smite the hell outta Marion's eatery.

Slowly, Dayton approached, his gun cemented in both hands. Didn't want to risk dropping it again.

The girl said, “Officer, he’s kinda had a bad day. He really doesn’t know what he’s doing.”

“Makes two of us, girl. I’m hungry, pissed off, been chasing him around town all night. And I don’t have a damn idea why! Drop the rock! Turn around!”

Christ, he really didn’t want to shoot the kid, especially not in the back. Media would love that, not to mention Dayton’s nagging conscience. And he still wasn’t sure the kid posed a threat, not one worthy of eating a bullet.

Inside Marion’s, Dayton spotted an older guy clutching a broom, watching the action. Ringside seat. Before bullets and rocks started flying, Dayton loosened one of his hands, tried to wave the old guy aside. The guy just looked at him quizzically, raised his hands: *Everyone crazy but me*?

Clearly the girl knew the Strawberry. More importantly, she seemed somewhat rational. Appeal to her. Dayton stuttered a few steps closer. Stopped, dipped a toe in the water to see if it’d calmed yet.

“Girl, how ’bout you talk some sense into your boyfriend? Tell him I’d rather not shoot him. Lotsa’ paperwork and headache. Maybe I can help, talk this out. He can be peas, I’ll be carrots. Get him to put the rock down.”

She nodded, a no-nonsense snap Dayton appreciated. Gently, she placed a hand on the frozen Strawberry’s shoulder. Leaned in, whispering something into his ear.

The Strawberry stiffened. He could go either way. Dayton prepped, ready to put one into his arm, maybe his leg if he could manage the shot. A little rusty on his target practice and his eyes weren’t what they used to be, though.

Village idiot style, the kid smiled at the girl as if remembering better days. He set the rock down, and turned around. But he only had eyes for the girl.

Thankfully Dayton didn't have to put his shooting prowess to the test. Likely would've come up with a failing grade.

To the girl, the Strawberry said, "He called me your boyfriend."

Jesus Christ. Now I gotta put up with puppy dog eyes and Hallmark moments.

Still wary, but grateful for the girl's intervention, Dayton pocketed his gun, traded it in for his wrist-ties. A call for peace, he raised a hand and walked toward the couple, his gun just a pull away. He probably didn't need to fret; the kid didn't know Dayton existed. Couldn't knock him out of the girl's orbit if he banged metal pots and pans next to his ear.

"I'm coming up to you now, son, with some plastic wrist restraints. Now…"

The hell with it. Kid couldn't hear him. Dayton straightened out of his TV cop pose and spoke directly to the girl. "You mind telling me what the hell's goin' on here tonight? Why's he in his tighty-whities?"

Apparently, Dayton said something to upset the Strawberry cart. Enraged, eyes wild and googly, the kid screamed, "I'm in my goddamn tighty-*whities* because Big Ben *made* me get him some chili to save my brother's *life*!"

Although it made no sense whatsoever, the girl gave Dayton a solemn nod, seriously nodding as if his outburst explained it all. But two things snagged Dayton's attention…

"Girl, did he say Big Ben put him up to this?"

Again, she nodded. She took a deep breath, throwing back her shoulders to speak but the Strawberry cut her off.

"You want Big Ben, right?" His eyes seemed clear now, a shortcut to saner times. He spoke calmly, the craziness tucked back inside his tighty-whities. "I can give you Big Ben. But you gotta help me. We need to do it *my* way."

"Son, I'd love nothin' more than to collar your pal, Big Ben. But I—"

"*Not* my pal."

"Looked mighty cozy on the sofa earlier tonight." Dayton knew they weren't friends, suspected the kid had been slumming, drug running maybe. Now he had doubts. But a lot rode on the line. He wanted to make sure he understood everything before going off crazy-like, allowing Landers to slip through legal whoopsies again.

"That's 'cause he made me sit next to him."

"Huh. You say you can give me Big Ben. I want him so bad, I can taste him." As a sour reminder, his stomach growled. "But he's tricky. I've had him before. Every time he gets off due to some fancy footwork by his lawyer or stupid technicalities. I need him wrapped up with a bow on top. Something no judge will—"

"How's murder sound?"

"Murder?" Dayton thought about it. "We talkin' heresay? Benji's got a big mouth on him."

"I'm talkin' murder that I witnessed. And I bet the body's still in his loft. Definitely the dead guy's DNA and the murder weapon."

Dayton scratched his goatee. Felt sweet tingles

feather down his back, his arms. Hoped like hell it wasn't a heart attack; that'd just be ironic in a too-sad way. "Strawberry, I think this might be the start of a beautiful friendship. Tell me more. And you got any pants?"

The kid's story was a corker, showcasing Benjamin Landers' sadistic side. When the Strawberry didn't make sense, the girl—Alicia—clarified things. One thing the kid made abundantly clear, though, was he demanded to get his brother outta the line of fire before any arrests were made.

Dayton said to Wendell, "I'm in. Before we go, though…" Dayton pulled out his badge, tapped it against the restaurant window. The restaurant's employee had been curiously watching them the entire time. "Open up, sir, I'm Officer Dayton Bookes. Official police business. I need two orders of chili to go. Fast as you can get 'em ready."

****

11:24 P.M.

Hunched over, one foot on the passenger side floorboard, Wendell prepared to slide into the Taurus.

Bookes didn't like the idea. "Whoa, hold on there, young blood! Whaddaya think you're doing?" His hand shot up.

"Um, getting in the car." To Wendell, it seemed pretty obvious.

"Nope. In the back seat." Dayton turned, reached behind him and grabbed a ratty-looking, frayed towel. "You ain't dirtyin' up my front seat in your skanky undies. Sit on the towel. Alicia rides shotgun."

Rather than arguing—they'd wasted far too much time already—Wendell crawled in back and Alicia snagged the front seat.

With only eight minutes to go, nerves gripped Wendell. He imagined Big Ben sharpening his knives, loading his guns while Drake sweated it out, tied to a chair, and sporting a rainbow of bruises.

"Damn, kid," said Bookes, looking in the rearview mirror, "you know you coulda' saved yourself a hella lotta trouble by just comin' to me in the first place."

"Couldn't. Against the rules."

Bookes pulled a classic double-take, first to the mirror, then over to Alicia. "The rules? What goddamn rules?" While tossing a thumb back toward Wendell, he asked Alicia, "He always go by the rules?"

Alicia nodded. "I think so."

"Bookes, we've only got eight minutes," said Wendell. "Can you make it in time?"

"No problem." He spoke around a mouthful of Marion's chili. "I could drive there with my eyes closed, been there so much."

Sudden panic seized Wendell, then squeezed. "Dammit… Ben's monitoring my progress! He'll know I cheated. Rode in a car!"

"Doubt that's a problem, Wendell. Hang on, lemme make sure." Bookes dialed a number, spoke quietly, quickly to the other party. Ended the call in twenty seconds. Wendell suspected he wanted to get back to his chili. "My buddies at City Hall picked up three of Ben's guys. They had a cell phone spoofed to follow the ankle monitor. Big Ben ain't watchin' you now."

"But he's got a guy, Dakeem, who's some sort of an electronics whiz or something. He—"

"I know Big Ben and—damn, this is good chili!—

he don't want to mess with that kinda thing. Too lazy. Or dumb. His crew does everything for him. Quit worryin', son."

Quit worrying. Easy for Bookes to say, he had nothing to lose. But Wendell and Drake's lives were on the line. So far they didn't even have a plan.

Bookes must've realized the same thing. "All right, let's work this out. We all know I can't just bully my way inside, ask to look in the back room. I mean, I suppose I could and all, but I'm not taking chances. Gotta be done by the book, every T crossed, every I dotted. This ain't gonna get tossed out of court." Another spoonful of chili didn't hinder Bookes' driving ability as he rushed through downtown. Based on the fast food wrappers swimming around Wendell's ankles, he imagined Bookes had lots of practice eating on the road.

"All right, now. Wendell, you want to go in first, deliver the chili, make sure your brother's safe. That right?"

"Yeah. I gotta get him outta there. Big Ben won't take this laying down."

"Ah, I ain't afraid of Big Ben." Bookes looked over his shoulder at Wendell, one hand on the steering wheel, the other coveting his chili. Miraculously, he kept the car in a straight line. "Besides, he's down three guys. Better odds for us."

"I guess." Odds still looked pretty bad from Wendell's point of view.

"I'm gonna need real cause, though, to come bustin' in. Good legal cause."

"I'll bring my brother up front, open the door, scream my head off about there being a dead body in back."

Again, Bookes served Wendell a death-defying backward look. "You're crazy if you think Ben's gonna let you and your bro just waltz on outta there. Crazy! You're a witness to a murder. He knows that. He's just been playin' you all night. Means to put you both six feet under. Damn." Bookes shook his head, stared into his chili. "Just crazy."

Had Wendell ever snatched a moment's peace tonight to consider the implication, he probably would've come to the same conclusion: Big Ben never had any intention of letting Wendell or Drake live.

A black hole of despair threatened to swallow Wendell. "So…what do we do?"

"I'm thinkin' on it." Although, honestly, Bookes' full attention appeared to be on his chili.

"We Trojan Horse their asses," said Alicia.

"How's that?" Bookes swept his gaze toward her, never on the road in front of him.

"We Trojan Horse our way inside." She looked at Bookes, then Wendell. Her hands went up, she shook her head, couldn't believe the idiots she shared the car with: *What's there to get?*

"Explain, girl. I ain't up on my Greek history."

Neither was Wendell, but he wasn't about to admit it. Alicia sighed, fed up with the Cro-Magnons in the car, and said, "Read a book sometime! Long story short, Ben's probably gonna suspect Wendell, definitely Bookes. They don't know me. I'll give Wendell a couple minutes, let him get back to his brother. Wendell, you lock down in that room with your bro, right?" Wendell nodded, wondering if there'd be an armed hood locked in there with them.

"I knock on the door," she continued. "They let me in. I say I wanna score some drugs. I make sure the door's unlocked—'cause Wendell said they keep it tight—then I go off like a siren. Bookes, you're out in the hall, come running in. You heard the scream, there's your probable cause. Boom! Wendell's brother's saved. Bookes gets the bad guy. We go home. Wendell puts on pants." She dusted her hands, all wrapped up and tidy.

Wendell just saw a bunch of unraveling. "No way, Alicia." He leaned forward, hands gripping the back of Alicia's seat. "You're not going in there. It's dangerous. They'll kill you—"

"Oh…my…God! Wendell, I thought you *heard* me earlier! I'm a big girl. I can take care of myself! I don't need your protection! We're in it to win it! Get used to it already!"

"It's a war-zone in that loft! They might—"

"Damn, it could work." Bookes kneaded his jowls, a meaty rubdown. "Look, son, I know you care about the girl and all. I get she's your girlfriend and every—"

"*Not* his girlfriend!" Alicia folded her arms.

"…thing, but it's a better plan than anything we got." Bookes crossed over the 12th Street Viaduct, turned into the Bottoms. "I'm not crazy about the idea either, sendin' in a couple of civilians. Things could go wrong. *Bad* wrong." Slowly, he entered Wendell's street. Ambled along at a turtle's pace. Then killed the headlights. "But it's gonna work. I'm gonna make it work. I'll be right outside, gun loaded. Like them, I ain't afraid to use it. Been a while." He parked along the street, couple of buildings away. Stroked his gun. A beam of moonlight captured his smile. "If any shooting starts, Wendell, you grab your brother, hit the floor in the back room. Stay there. And, Alicia? You get the hell outta there soon as I come barrelin' in like Liam Neeson. We're here. Let's do it." He killed the ignition.

****

11:31 P.M.

Short of breath after the three flights of stairs, Wendell pounded on the door. He stood proudly in his underwear. The cardboard container of chili weighed down the paper bag in his hand but he felt like hoisting it over his head, his winning trophy for completing the grueling marathon. Yet the fight wasn't over yet. Mentally, he prepared to break some rules.

Again, the bass line reverberated through the floor, exploded out of the room once the door opened. A guy Wendell hadn't seen before stood before him, decked out with jewelry, sideways ballcap and shorts so low they may as well've been socks.

"Yeah?"

Wendell held up the sack. "Big Ben sent me on a chili run."

Nothing. Blank stare, a wall of ice.

"Tell him it's Wendy."

The door closed. Opened again. The music abruptly stopped.

"I'll be goddamned, Wendy!" Big Ben sat on his sofa, alone for a change. But next to the sofa stood Dakeem. "You made it with…" He rearranged his neck clock to look at it. Moved it back and forth like his eyesight was going. "One minute to spare! Wendy, the king of suspense!" His large hands clapped, gunfire in the spacious loft. "Give it up for Wendy, boys! Didn't think you were gonna come through."

Dakeem clapped, but remained grim.

Big Ben waved him over. “Damn, boy, I been starvin’. Gimme that chili.”

“What about my brother?”

“What about him?”

“You said I bring you chili. Hit the deadline. You let us go.” Wendell stood his ground, holding the bag of chili hostage. He supposed it came down to how much Ben wanted to eat.

Serious now, Big Ben motioned for Wendell to come forward. “I said bring me my damn chili.”

“Not until—*umph…*” Low-Shorts, the guy who let Wendell in, grabbed the back of his neck, aided him toward the sofa.

Wendell handed the bag to Ben. Ben tore the bag apart, flipped the container’s top off, unwrapped the plastic spork, and dove in. Piled high on the spork, Ben shoveled the chili into his mouth. His smile dropped. “It’s *cold*, Wendy.”

“What do you expect? After running across town? You got a microwave, I assume. Use it.”

His cold eyes locked on Wendell. Ben bagged the chili and tossed it to Dakeem, who. rushed to the kitchen—master of the microwave apparently one of his many electronic talents.

Wendell stared down Big Ben. His throat dried out. His knees weakened. But he wouldn’t be intimidated.

“Damn, Wendy, you grow some balls while you were gone?” asked Ben.

Wendell thought about it, and realized he had. Much less afraid of confrontation—even potentially deadly confrontation—than he’d been two hours ago. The consequences he supposed of his trauma, his “walkabout.” In a way, he owed Big Ben his thanks.

Nah.

"We had a deal, Ben. I want to see my brother. Then you let us go." Big words. Wendell tried to square his body up to match them: shoulders back, chin up, gaze never wavering.

"Where's Little Ben and the others? You do somethin' to them, Wendy? Call the cops or somethin' maybe? Gotta make sure the rules stay in place. Be like livin' in the Old West—we don't have rules to abide by."

"Haven't seen your guys. Not since an hour ago when Jiggy tried to whip me. Doesn't matter. Why don't you own *your* rules, Ben?"

"You forget your place, Wendy? That it?" Big Ben shot out of the sofa, filling the loft with his largesse. He glided around the coffee table, and stood before Wendell, emphasizing his height.

"My place is anywhere but here," said Wendell. "I want my brother. Deal's a deal. And from now on, you leave us both alone." Really, Wendell was in no position to sit at the head of the bargaining table. He realized that. But the words just flowed as naturally as going to the bathroom, poured right out of him, and he really didn't need to be thinking about *that* right now.

When Ben said nothing, Wendell doubted himself, his chicken persona coming back to roost. Nothing more than false bravado, cockiness enabled by his many narrow escapes tonight. Just dumb, blind luck.

But he couldn't back down now. Any minute now Alicia would knock on the door. He had to get to the back room, to his brother.

Ben turned to Low-Shorts. "You believe this guy?"

"No respect, G."

Timp.

Ben thrust a finger into Wendell's chest. Wendell bobbled, but like a wind puppet, he settled back into place. And said nothing.

Over the unsettling quiet, the moment before the storm, the microwave hummed in the kitchen. Wendell's nerves sizzled.

Ben landed both hands on Wendell's chest. Wendell went back, thrusting his arms about like a punk rocker unleashed. He wouldn't give Ben the satisfaction of falling. A small victory.

"Show some respect, Wendy!" Ben's exterior cracked, Wendell the ice breaker. His nostrils inflated. His bloodshot eyes shifted wildly. Scary, *murderously* wildly.

Maybe I pushed a little too far?

"Let's start over, Ben. You have your chili. I want my brother. Peace. I'm going back there now to get him."

Wendell brushed by Ben. Ben swung around, roped an arm around Wendell's neck. Wendell clawed at his arm. Ben's grip tightened, drawing Wendell back into his unloving embrace.

In Wendell's ear, he said, "You just dug your own grave, Wendy."

Bang, bang, bang!

Crap! Not yet, Alicia!

"Goddamn airport terminal in here tonight." Ben's grip loosened slightly, but he kept Wendell close. "See who it is, Ty."

Ty (aka "Low-Shorts") nodded, trotted over to the door, and slung back the inset window. "Yeah?" he yelled.

"Hey!" Though muted, Alicia's indistinguishable voice. "I'm lookin' for a party boost. Heard you got the best around."

Ty left her hanging, and informed his boss, "Some hottie chick. Lookin' to hold."

Ben jerked his chin. "Who sent her?"

"Who sent you?" relayed Ty.

Pause. Long pause. Achingly long pause. Finally, "I'm a friend of Jiggy's."

"Ask her she's a cop," said Ben.

"You a cop?"

"Hell, no!" Alicia shouted, loud and clear.

Ty looked back toward Ben. Wendell, still caught in Ben's stranglehold, scrambled to come up with a backup, go-for-broke plan.

Ben said, "How hot is she?"

Ty nodded. "Pretty damn hot."

"Let her in." Ben thrust his other arm around Wendell's belly.

"What about him?" Ty pointed toward Wendell.

"If she's just lookin' to party, Wendy won't matter. Maybe we'll have some fun."

Dark visions of "fun" trainwrecked Wendell's mind. He wouldn't let it happen, especially not to Alicia.

But, one way or another, they had to get the door open. Time to improvise and hope like hell Bookes was ready.

Ty drew across the chainlock, and let it drop. *Tchkkk*. Threw back the deadbolt. *Chok*. Flipped the lock set within the doorknob. *Fitch*.

Three stupid locks!

The door swung back. Ty stepped aside. At once,

small and unassuming, yet somehow confident like she belonged there, Alicia strode in. Nonchalantly, she took in the loft, her gaze wandering. Briefly, it lingered on Wendell. Then moved on. Much better actor than Wendell'd ever be.

"Who's in charge?" She jumped slightly when Ty threw the locks back in place behind her.

"That'd be me, sweet thing." With Ben's mouth next to Wendell's ear, he heard Ben's shark-like smile widen, wet and gummy.

Unimpressed, Alicia said, "Whaddaya got?" Then her gaze fell back on Wendell. "What's this all about?"

"Wendy? Don't worry 'bout him. We're ol' friends. Stick around, baby, maybe we can have a good time."

"Already got good waitin' for me, full up on good. I'm here for something better than good, maybe for my nose."

Ben finally relinquished his hold on Wendell. Stayed shoulder to shoulder with him. "Ty, go get it."

"Nuh uh. No way. I only deal with the head guy," said Alicia. "You want my money, you talk to me."

With absolutely no idea what Alicia was up to, Wendell hoped she had a better handle on plotting under pressure than he did. Big Ben remained quiet. Wendell waited to see which way he'd tip.

Big Ben's laughter nudged him to the softer side of psycho. "Fine, baby. Be back in a minute. Then we'll talk. Maybe get cozy on my sofa. You like what you see?" Ben lifted his arms, displaying his digs.

Her nose wrinkled. "Seen better."

Hardly a man's world, Big Ben tolerated Alicia's lip just fine.

"Ty, keep an eye on Wendy here." Ben yelled at Dakeem in the kitchen, "Goddamn, man, how long's it take to heat up chili?"

"Like you taught me. Stir, heat, stir, heat, stir—"

"Good thing you know your way 'round tech stuff, you ain't nothin' in the kitchen." Ben vanished down the hallway toward the back.

Interpreting his boss' instructions quite literally, Ty bellied up to Wendell, his gaze never flinching, let alone blinking.

While Ty only had eyes for Wendell, Wendell noticed what Alicia had up her sleeve. A dangerous move.

Inch by inch, Alicia backed toward the door. With her hands behind her, her elbows jut out in minute motions.

Ty shot her a look. She froze, and smiled. Hard to resist a smile like hers. Ty smiled back. But Wendell needed to gain back Ty's undying devotion.

Small talk not his forte, Wendell flew blindly. "So, Ty, can I call you Ty? Or do you prefer Tyrone or, ah, Tylliver? How long have you worked for Big Ben?"

A corner of Ty's mouth went up, just enough to let a little growl escape. Ready to take a bite out of Wendell. But Wendell had succeeded in winning back his full, undivided attention.

"You like it here? Hey, I've always wondered if guys like Big Ben have a full benefits package. I know that might sound kinda dumb and everything, but, really, in your line of work, you might end up in the hospital a lot and…"

Over his meandering monologue, Wendell heard a little sound, a tiny tick: the knob lock set free. He raised his voice, jazzed up his word flow.

"…well, do you get insurance? Or does Big Ben pay for your hospital bills? That's gotta be it, right? I'm bettin' Big Ben makes huge bank, right? Sure, he…"

Alicia coughed. Over it, Wendell distinguished another diminutive click, the deadbolt unlocked.

Ty swung his attention toward her. She dropped her hands to her side. Unmistakably shaking. Wendell's monologue dried up. His heart hammered. Not for himself, for Alicia's welfare.

"Hey! Get away from the door!" Ty left Wendell's side, and stormed toward Alicia. "The hell you doin'?"

"Nothing. Just chillin', bein' cool!" Her smile rose, so did her hands. The friendly gestures failed to ward off his approach. He raced toward her.

Alicia wheeled. Fidgeted with the chain lock. Her fingers grasped it, pulled it halfway across the slide.

Over the kitchen bar counter, Dakeem looked on with curious indifference.

Ty gripped Alicia's arm, yanking her back. With his other hand, he grabbed her hair.

Wendell didn't think about it, just raged into hero mode. For a murderous thug, Big Ben had a surprising lack of weapons on display. The coffee table looked heavy. Didn't matter, not one bit. Adrenaline coursed through Wendell. He swept the table free of a handful of remotes, jerked it to his waist. Couldn't quite get it high enough, not for what he needed. *Improvise.* Arm muscles strained. With the table as a chest shield, he rushed Ty.

Wendell's battle cry ripped through the loft. He rammed the table into Ty's back. Ty dropped his violent grip on Alicia, and going with good instincts, she spun left along the wall. Wendell sandwiched the table into Ty. They bounced off the door and crashed to the ground, both of them grunting from the impact. Struggling to stay aboard the table, Wendell body-surfed while Ty ineffectively swept fists out to the side.

"The hell's goin' on?" Dakeem leaned over the kitchen counter, watching the struggling men.

"Your guy went crazy," screamed Alicia, "and attacked me!"

Because of Wendell's own weight defeating him, the table lifted only a couple inches when Wendell yanked at it. Wendell used it anyway, bashed it down. Hardly an effective blow, but he repeated the move. Bigger, stronger than Wendell, Ty pushed back. The table bucked. Wendell rolled off.

A ballet dancer gone 'roid rage, Alicia jerked her knee up, then crunched her foot down on the table. Beneath it, Ty moaned. A winning sound.

Spack.

Launched from the kitchen, a bullet zipped over Alicia's head.

"Jesus!"

The projectile thwacked into an ornamental sun god sculpture on the wall. With a resounding clang, it fell to the floor and wobbled on the hardwood floor.

Wendell clambered up. He wrenched the table off Ty, wrestled it up on end. An ineffective shield against bullets, but the best they had.

"Alicia, behind me! Get the lock free!"

Wendell scooted forward, clearing the door, leaving Alicia room to operate. He stepped over Ty, his legs wobbly. He strong-armed the table up, hunkered behind it. A bullet shaved the top of the table, splintered the wood. He couldn't duck lower, no leeway, his feet already exposed.

Alicia scrabbled at the lock and pulled it free. Ty lay in the way, preventing the door from opening.

"Dammit, we gotta move him!"

Wendell popped the table up onto one knee, trying to free up an arm. Ty latched onto his ankle. Like a rabid dog, he wouldn't let go. On one leg, Wendell hopped. His entire body felt ready to implode. His muscles had never taken such a beating. The table tottered, he caught it, and fought to keep it up. It now weighed more than Wendell, heavier by the second.

The door popped open, then bounced back shut when it hit Ty.

"Police! Open up!" yelled Bookes. He pushed the door open again, leaning into it, face through the open crack. "Goddammit! Open the door!"

Another gunshot cracked. It hit a target, soft and wet sounding. But there was nothing soft about the jagging pain stabbing through Wendell's left hand. He jerked back his hand. The table dropped, clopping Ty's forehead. He released Wendell's ankle, out for the count.

Wendell nearly joined him. Dakeem's bullet had pureed his pinky finger to a bloody mess. Wendell swooned. He toppled forward. His knees crunched down, but he managed his good hand out to prevent banging fully onto the floor.

Stay with it! Don't pass out!

Mercifully a lousy shot, Dakeem launched another bullet over Wendell's head. On his knees, Wendell grabbed one of Ty's arms. He focused his strength, tuned out the gunfire, ignored his wound, and dragged

Ty. The unconscious man slid a foot away from the door. Still not enough door clearance. Exhausted from the effort, Wendell buckled.

Alicia didn't scream for Bookes. But Wendell sure did, even if he didn't have to now. Pretty easy, actually, once he glanced at his finger again.

Faster than Wendell's addled mind could follow, Alicia grabbed Ty's legs. Aided by Bookes pushing, she cleared the path. The door flung open. Alicia rolled with it, dove for cover behind the open door.

Bookes stormed in, filled the doorway. He tottered in front of Ty's body, his arms windmilling. When he saw Wendell on the floor, he froze. Then a bullet whizzed by him and woke him up in a hurry.

Fast for a large man, he hopped over Ty. He dashed toward the kitchen, gun up and unleashing a seemingly inexhaustible slew of bullets. Dakeem dropped, bunkering behind the bar counter.

From the back, another man ran out, his gun jerking up and down. With no clear target in sight, a leap before you look sort, he sprayed bullets in an arc, far above Wendell. On the other hand, Alicia, upright and glued to the wall, made an easy target.

Wendell worked fast. He sat up, and punched Ty in the groin just to make sure he'd stay down. He patted down his shorts, found what he needed. A gun.

He'd never fired a gun before—never wanted to, really—but figured he'd learn now in a literal trial by fire. He flipped a lever. He took aim at the new guy, who apparently hadn't spotted him yet. Wendell pulled the trigger. Definitely not like the movies, no satisfying roar, not even a kickback. Nothing. He fumbled, found another switch, flicked it. His good arm swung up and he fired.

The gun whiplashed, sending him flat on his back again. But the gun decided to continue firing, a mind of its own. Bullets spackled the ceiling, redecorating the walls. A vase exploded. Clearly off-target, but enough to send the new gunman scuttling for refuge somewhere.

A cacophonic choir of voices screamed, each one trying to outshout the other.

Wendell loudest of all. "*Alicia*! Get out!"

No fool, she ducked, swung around the door.

Bullets popped over her head. She shrieked and dropped. *Not hit, please, God, don't let her be hit.* On hands and knees, she crawled into the hallway.

At the kitchen counter, Bookes and Dakeem were embroiled in a strange stand-off, trading bullets over the bar separating them, feet apart, but bullets aimed wildly off. Just adding more shrapnel throughout the loft. His back against the wall, Bookes sat on the floor, legs spread apart. Tired. Gun smoking in hand. Above him, Dakeem popped up. With a knee on top of the counter, moving very quietly, he leaned over. Dakeem lowered his gun hand over the edge before Wendell could shout a warning. Bookes didn't bother looking, just shot upward. His finger extremely happy to be on the trigger, he didn't let up. Bullets shredded Dakeem's hand, a red burst of destruction. The gun bounced into Bookes' lap. Dakeem, his eyes rolling up, dropped behind the bar.

On hands and knees, Bookes crawled across the loft. He stopped at the sofa set next to the hallway. As if his knees were giving him fits, he grimaced as he worked up into a squat. He probably hadn't been in a squat since high school gym.

Wendell slithered across the floor, away from the hallway opening. Past Ty, who appeared still unconscious, a moot player. Wendell worked up on a knee. When he tried to get to his feet, his left pinky brushed the floor. Pain shot through him, nearly sending him back down. But he had a job to finish.

Bookes' mouth formed a definitive "No." Wendell ignored him. He crouch-walked—more like waddled—toward the opposite side of the hallway entrance and took up wall space across from Bookes. He needed to see what they were up against, no telling how many men were back there.

Down low, Wendell peeked around the corner, and yelled "Hey!" into the hallway. Gunfire ripped over him. He jerked back and embraced the wall. Next to Bookes, bullets whiffed into the arm of the upholstery. His arms jacked up and he went down again. Foam and leather flew.

Bookes glowered at Wendell, mouthing a savage stream of obscenities. Belly on the ground, double-fisting guns, Bookes used his elbows to crawl just enough to peek around the sofa. Then he laid down an army's worth of bullets down the hallway.

Fire returned on Bookes.

"God *damn*," he screamed.

Head down, he retreated. Tables split, fell over. Mirrors shattered. One of the TVs broke free from its wall-nook, the resultant crash monstrous. Above, the chandelier tinkled, swung like a pendulum. Prisms fell. A large chunk of ceiling plaster plummeted like a bomb. Miniature clouds rose from it.

Bookes got to his knees, struggled to his feet using

the sofa as support. Sweat rolled off him like a man in a sauna.

Wendell dared another glimpse around the corner. Nothing. All quiet. Except he saw the shooter's sneaker tips poking out of a doorway. Hard to miss neon green.

Bookes shook his head, dumbfounded, a little uncertain. Shaking loose courage for his next move. Or praying. Wendell waved at Bookes, pointed toward the floor, his feet, drew a rectangle in the air, then gestured toward the hallway. He had no idea if the cop had read him correctly or not; the only thing Bookes looked like he wanted to read was Wendell his rights.

Bookes took a deep breath and dove in. One gun raised, the other aimed from his waist, he walked sideways down the hall, close to the wall. Sideways or not, he still made a barn-sized target. He needed backup.

The floorboard creaked—the first sign of old age in Ben's loft—as Wendell took a step down the hall. Bookes started, looked back. He slashed his hand down, his face folded into ulcer-inducing anger.

Bookes stopped when he saw the sneaker tips. Casually, he lowered a gun. Pasted a series of bullets into the guy's feet. The gunman yelped, fell back with a thump. Bleeding sneakers stuck out from the doorway.

Wendell just waited. For what? He didn't know. But his brother was still in that room. His bane, his partner in dumb, ultimately his responsibility.

Bookes stepped between the guy's legs, lost his balance a little, then righted himself. Headed toward the back room, the true finish line of the nightmare that wouldn't end.

With a light touch, Bookes lifted his thumb and

forefinger from a gun and tried the closed door knob. It twisted. Swung open an inch. Bookes hesitated. Breathing hard. He swung up a jacket sleeve, and drew it across his brow. Set his mouth tight.

Like a parent trying to coax a kid out of hiding, he said, "Landers? It's me, Bookes. What say you come out, nice and easy now. No guns. We'll just talk. You and me. Palsies." Bookes stepped back against the wall. Ready for unfriendly fire.

"Step off, fat man!" Bullets riddled the door, ending the conversation.

Noticing Wendell still in the game, Bookes whispered, "Call 911!"

Wendell's hands went up: *No phone*.

But in the distance, sirens cut through the silence. Friendly banshees. Louder and closer. No doubt Alicia's work.

Frustrated, Bookes again shook his head. Possibly thinking of that pension at the end of the rainbow. A rainbow soon to be blood-spattered.

Wendell started this. Actually, Drake did. But Wendell needed to finish it. He didn't know how. Had no clue. But if he lingered too long, he'd probably wuss out. Realize he was about to embark on a suicide mission. Kind of a strong argument.

Don't think about it. Just do it. Make up your own rules. Don't play by anyone else's.

He tucked Ty's gun into the back waistband of his tighty-whities. The gun felt cold, a little dangerous, next to his bare bottom, but it was the first time all night he appreciated his choice of underwear. They didn't call them "tight" for nothing; the skin-hugging elastic band kept the gun snug.

Boldly, he walked down the hall. Bookes flung back his arm. As if the cop didn't exist, Wendell passed him, afraid if he looked at him he'd buckle beneath the experienced cop's steely gaze. He gripped the doorknob.

"Ben, it's me, Wendy. I'm comin' in, 'kay? Don't shoot. Obviously I don't have a gun. You can search me if you want. But really…where in hell am I gonna hide anything, right?"

Ben's voice pitched a little higher than usual. "Wendy, you crazy! Why in hell you wanna come in here?

Well, it's not a "no."

"I just want to see my brother. If he's okay, you can take both of us hostage. You can walk outta here a free man."

"Bullshit! What about Bookes?"

"I'll tell him to back off. He won't put civilians in the line of fire." Sounded good, at least.

Bookes narrowed his eyes, madder than hell.

"Tell Bookes to go to the kitchen. And stay there. You grab his gun, bring it to me. Hand it to me butt first."

"I'll see what I can do." Wendell held his hand out. Bookes almost handed over the gun he'd liberated from Dakeem, then reclaimed it. He pointed toward his chest, held his police model up, mouthed: *I'll do it*.

Calmness comforted Wendell, a cozy blanket of security. The Zen of not being neurotic.

Bookes gripped Wendell's arm and whispered, "Just wait for the cops, dammit. You're gonna get everyone in that room killed."

Wendell said nothing. Time for a cheap ploy. He

jerked his head down the hallway, eyes wide and scared as if he saw someone. Bookes bought it, looked. Easier than taking candy from a baby, Wendell liberated Dakeem's gun.

"Goddammit…" Bookes hissed.

Wendell patted the air. Nodded smugly. Turned, showed Bookes his backside, maybe the only one in Downtown, KC who hadn't yet seen it tonight. Then he pointed down the hallway, banishing Bookes to the kitchen. Bookes wouldn't budge, not that Wendell really expected him to.

Improvise.

"Bookes is in the kitchen, Ben. I'm coming in."

Nothing. Wendell swallowed. Closed his eyes. Placed his wounded left hand on the door, his right hand free for a quick draw. Pushed. The door opened.

The three of them sat on the bed, Drake in the middle, Ben's bimbo on the other side. For added impetus to behave, Ben's gun pressed against Drake's temple. Regardless, Drake had his arm around the girl's shoulders, for God's sake. "Community chest," maybe.

Duct tape kept Drake's big mouth shut. Rope bound his ankles together. Weird they left his hands free.

And hooray for evidential corpses! Napoleon's body leaned against the corner of the room like a replaced room carpet.

"The hell you playin' at anyway, Wendy?" Ben scooted off the bed, sending it rocking. A waterbed for his hostages.

The girl cried out for no discernible reason, just a small cluck. Surely she'd grown used to Ben's behavior by now. Streaks of mascara rode her cheeks.

Through his non-inflamed eye, Drake looked up at his younger brother, mumbled something unintelligible. Hardly a first.

Ben came at Wendell, gun locked at arm's length. He planted the cold barrel directly above Wendell's Adam's apple. As much as Wendell wanted to swallow, he was afraid it'd trigger the gun.

"I'm not the one dying here tonight," said Ben. "You playin', Wendy? Planning something with Bookes?"

Wendell didn't think about it. Didn't talk about it. He answered Ben's questions with action. Much louder than words, after all.

Wendell's left arm—his wounded hand—jabbed up between them, a desperate buffer. Fast and fluid, Wendell's upper arm followed through on a roundabout trajectory, banged into Ben's gun hand, knocked it aside. Ben's gun pointed down, rocked a bullet into the floor. Wendell's right arm windmilled in the opposite direction, snagged the gun butt, drew it up and around. Landed it on Ben's temple.

Ben blinked. His eyes shifted toward the left, toward the gun. His head went back, his chest filled with air. Preparing to do something dangerous.

The girl shrieked. Again.

Drake scooted forward, bouncing on the bed. Arms out, he dropped over the side. His chin anchored onto the floor. He snagged Ben's legs and yanked. Wendell twisted. Ben fell forward. The gun clattered out of his hand.

Wendell tossed his gun to Drake. Ever the athlete and even from the floor disadvantage, Drake caught it. Turned it around on Ben.

Wendell dropped down onto his knees, making sure they ground in nice and sharp on Ben's back.

"Goddammit, Wendy, get offa' me!"

Wendell grabbed Ben's ears and thwacked his head against the floor. "My name's *not* Wendy, dammit! I'm *not* the friggin' hamburger girl! I'm sure as hell not a *Strawberry*! And I'm not your whipping boy! I'm Wendell Worthy!"

Ben bucked up onto hands and knees, and tossed Wendell over. Fist pulled back to hammer, Ben launched on top of Wendell. The weight, the muscle advantage were all Ben's. Wendell fought. He knocked aside Ben's arm, his fist deflecting onto Ben's chest. Hurt like hell, too. Muscles of steel seemed to reinforce Ben's chest.

With a guttural growl, Wendell turned savage. He landed a bull's-eye into Ben's throat. Stunned, Ben's hands flew to his throat. Wendell shoved him off and traded spots. Tossing slaps, pinching, hair-pulling, head-butting, groin-punching, everything he could muster, nothing he considered; not the manliest fight ever, but one he meant to win. And he absolutely hated rolling around with a guy, fighting for his life in his underwear.

Ben's arms went flat on the floor. His hands clawed up, fingernails scratched at the floor. And Wendell kept delivering the pain, using everything in his arsenal. Which didn't amount to much other than one good hand and his forehead.

He looked up, glimpsed Bookes smiling, an expression the cop hadn't worn since he dug into his chili. It would've been nice had Bookes notified Wendell of his arrival.

Between punches, Wendell yelled, "You enjoying this, Bookes?"

"Kinda," said Bookes. "But playtime's over. Time to get up. Let me do my damn job." Bookes didn't say anything else, just swung his plastic cuffs around a finger. Enjoying the show.

Frankly, Wendell couldn't be happier to get up. Glad to leave his long night of crime and punishment behind.

More than glad to tear the tape from Drake's mouth and make sure it hurt. *Bad.*

"Ow! Goddamn, Wendell, took you long enough!" He looked his brother over, finally acknowledging Wendell's shoddy, beaten, near-naked appearance. "What happened to you, brah? You okay?"

Wendell sighed. "Long story. Tell you later. Are *you* okay?"

Drake shrugged. "Yeah, dude, no sweat. Really, they didn't treat me that crappy. I spent most of the time playing cards with Gwen here!" Gwen smiled.

Wendell's eyelids fluttered, trying to spin winning logic. He studied the tape still in his hand. Without saying a word, he unpeeled it from his fingers. Splotched it back across his brother's mouth. Wendell left the room as Drake mumbled behind him.

He stumbled down the hallway. Cops rushed by him, giving him no more than a sideways glance. Just another freak show, hardly the main event in the back room.

As he left the hallway, medics, too, hustled through the door. Alicia stood aside. Arms folded. Barking directions, pointing at things.

She saw Wendell. Opened her arms and ran to him.

They embraced. Wendell didn't mind the throbbing pain in his pinky, not one bit, as he held onto her.

"You okay?" she asked.

"I think so." Actually, he didn't really think so. But there'd be plenty time to think about that later. "How're you?"

"Nothin' wrong with me." She smiled. "There's an ambulance waiting for you. Can you make it downstairs by yourself? These guys are running around like chickens with their heads cut off." She dismissed the chaos with a downward hand slash.

"Yeah, let's go."

A medic greeted them at the door, and held it open for them. She eyed Wendell's hand. Blood dripped from it. "Let's get you to the ambulance."

After they loaded Wendell, Alicia hiked up a leg on the ambulance stairs, ready to embark.

"Sorry," said the medic, "only family allowed."

"What? Dammit, how do you know I'm not family? Just 'cause—"

"It's okay," said Wendell. "She's my girlfriend."

The medic softened. "That right?"

"That's right," Alicia answered while boarding. She snuggled up to Wendell, and held his hand, his good hand.

Before Wendell passed out, the soundtrack of his story played out. A swelling horn section, celestial trumpets, all brought to a deliriously feverish pitch of love.

And…fade out.

A word about the author…

Stuart R. West is a lifelong resident of Kansas, which he considers both a curse and a blessing. It's a curse because…well, it's Kansas. But it's great because…well, it’s Kansas. Lots of cool, strange and creepy things happen in the Midwest, and Stuart takes advantage of them in his books. Call it “Kansas Noir.” Stuart writes thrillers, horror, and mysteries usually tinged with humor, both for adult and young adult audiences.

Stuart spent 25 years in the corporate sector and had to bail, splitting his time between writing and real estate. He’s married to a professor of pharmacy (who greatly appreciates the fact he cooks dinner for her every night) and has a 31-year-old daughter who’s dabbling in the nefarious world of banking.

If you're still reading this, you may as well head on over to Stuart's blog at: http://stuartrwest.blogspot.com/ It's what all the cool kids are doing.

Thank you for purchasing
this publication of The Wild Rose Press, Inc.

For questions or more information
contact us at
info@thewildrosepress.com.

The Wild Rose Press, Inc.
www.thewildrosepress.com

www.ingramcontent.com/pod-product-compliance
Lightning Source LLC
LaVergne TN
LVHW050628100826
845148LV00011B/1780

* 9 7 8 1 5 0 9 2 5 4 1 1 8 *